Title: Elle Campbell Wins Their Weekend

Author: Ben Kahn

On-Sale Date: October 17, 2023

Format: Jacketed Hardcover

ISBN: 978-1-338-81530-6 || Price: $18.99 US

Ages: 8–12

Grades: 3–7

LOC Number: Available

Length: 272 pages

Trim: 5 1/2 x 8 1/4 inches

Classification: Juvenile Fiction:
Humorous Stories /
LGBTQ+ /
People & Places; United States; General /
Social Themes; Friendship

---------------- *Additional Formats Available* --------------

Ebook ISBN: Available

D1411763

Scholastic Press
An Imprint of Scholastic Inc.
557 Broadway, New York, NY 10012
For information, contact us at:
tradepublicity@scholastic.com

ELLE CAMPBELL WINS THEIR WEEKEND

ELLE CAMPBELL WINS THEIR WEEKEND

BEN KAHN

Scholastic Press / New York

Library of Congress Cataloging-in-Publication Data available

ISBN 978-1-338-81530-6

10 9 8 7 6 5 4 3 2 1   23 24 25 26 27

Printed in the U.S.A.   66

First edition, October 2023

Book design by Stephanie Yang

To everyone who found themselves
in stories.

ONE

There were so many useful ways that Elle Campbell could have started their day. They could have gotten an early start on brushing their teeth and getting dressed for school. Heavens knew it took them long enough to pick out the perfect androgynous outfit. They could have done jumping jacks and begun their morning with a little healthy exercise. Heck, even staying in bed and squeezing their eyes tightly shut until the alarm blared would have been a more productive use of Elle's time.

Instead, they groggily pulled themself out of bed and made a beeline for their computer to read the latest comments about Elle's favorite show—*Phantom Thief.*

The show was about supernatural thieves who pulled daring

1

heists all across time and space, and was just about Elle's favorite thing in the whole wide world.

Elle usually loved talking to other fans, but today their mood only soured as they read a long chain of comments attacking their favorite episode, "Wolf Heart."

'Wolf Heart' is the best, most important Phantom Thief episode in years, and anyone who doesn't see that is a FOOL! Elle typed fiercely in response.

The "Wolf Heart" episode had introduced the current protagonist, the witty nonbinary hacker who had changed Elle's life completely. The character had given them the knowledge and the courage to come out as nonbinary.

Why didn't these internet twerps understand that? Why couldn't they realize how *important* it was to them?

Elle spun around in their desk chair and surveyed the room appreciatively. Nearly every inch of it was covered in memorabilia from the show. There were the *Phantom Thief* posters on the wall, the *Phantom Thief* figurines that stood atop a bookshelf filled with *Phantom Thief* paperbacks and graphic novels. Next to their computer with the *Phantom Thief* desktop wallpaper was a picture frame of Elle cosplaying as a character from *Phantom Thief* at a local convention.

"Elle! Time to get ready, hon!" shouted Elle's mother. There was no corner of the house in which one could hide from the bellowing of Susan Campbell. Yodelers and banshees traveled the world over to learn her secrets of vocal projection.

"I'm getting ready, Mom!" Elle called out even as they remained in their office chair, legs folded like a contortionist. Elle had read online about the stereotype that queer people couldn't sit in chairs properly and had decided to embrace it.

"No, you're not! You're arguing with strangers on the internet, aren't you? Stoppit!"

"It's not *arguing*, Mom. It's civilized discussions on the pressing cultural issues of our day."

Suddenly, the door to Elle's room burst open and Susan Campbell flung herself through, doing her best impression of a character from some 90s sitcom that she'd tried—and failed—to get Elle to watch.

"Honey, I love you, but you need to stop arguing with strangers about which characters should kiss which other characters and get ready for school."

Elle pouted. They hadn't been arguing about fictional couples. Well, not *this* time at least. Most of the time, yes. But not this time!

"Please don't give me that face, Elle." Sue's expression softened. "I love you, and I'm so proud of you and want you to always be your truest self, but ever since you came out it takes you three times as long to get ready in the morning. So get going before you miss the bus."

Elle finally unfolded their legs to slither out of their office chair.

"That's just 'cause fashion *makes sense* now. There's so much more to choose from and decide on! I want to look right and look cute, but it's so much work and it takes *forever*, ya know?"

Sue smiled, brushing aside a lock of her long red hair. "You don't have to tell me, I've been at this a lot longer than you have. Welcome to the world of beauty, kiddo! Now get dressed and put on whichever makeup you like today," she called as she left Elle's room, closing the door behind her. "You do it fast, then I got toast and eggs ready for you. You go slow, then I'm shoving you out the door with just one of those oat and grain bars that turn into a literal mountain of crumbs."

Elle opened their closet. In just a few months, what had once been a wardrobe full of ripped jeans and logo T-shirts had given way to skirts, blouses, and button-downs in loud colors and patterns. Elle's eyes hovered over a jade-green dress. It had been Elle's first dress and was still their favorite. And to them, it looked even better now that their fiery red hair hung nearly to their shoulders. But now that it was time to actually put it on, they were second-guessing themself.

Wearing a dress always meant getting more stares from people at school. Even the excitement of wearing a pretty dress tended to fade after enough mocking looks and judgmental sneers. Some days Elle felt strong enough to fight the whole world . . . and some days they didn't.

Elle passed the dress and rifled through the hangers until they got to their button-downs. The shirts were loud and colorful, most covered in floral patterns. But still, they were a touch more masculine than the dress, and would garner less attention.

Elle felt a little pang of guilt for not choosing the dress, like they weren't being true to themself. But they couldn't help but smile when they buttoned up their shirt and looked in the mirror. The dark blue fabric was covered with bright purple and green leaves, flowers, and cacti. The combination of the colorful shirt with their long hair made Elle confident that no stranger on the street would even be able to tell what gender they were. And that's exactly how Elle liked it. If they had to be confused about their gender, they were gonna make everyone else just as confused about it too.

Elle moved over to a shelf crowded with baubles and accessories and put on a pair of pink flower clip-on earrings. Elle knew they shouldn't be vain, but they couldn't help but feel joyous as they stood in front of the mirror. Elle couldn't have imagined being this person even a few months ago. Sometimes it still didn't feel real.

Elle's moment of celebration was interrupted by Susan's powerful voice making its way into their room. "The kitchen for eggs is closing in ten . . . nine . . . eight . . ."

"I'm coming down right now!" Elle shouted back, having more than inherited their mother's powerful set of vocal cords. They took one final moment to adjust their collar *just so* before racing out of their room.

"How you want your eggs? Scrambled or hard-boiled?" Sue asked as Elle strode into the kitchen.

"Uhh . . . I dunno. Scrambled?" Sue handed Elle a plate with toast and two eggs that were neither scrambled nor hard-boiled.

"Well, too bad, because I already did 'em sunny-side up!" Elle rolled their eyes and took a satisfying bite out of the toast and eggs. Already sitting at the table was Sue's newest boyfriend, Jerome. Elle was used to their mother dating, but at two years, Jerome was by far the longest-lasting relationship that Elle could remember— so maybe not so new after all. But admitting that Jerome wasn't new meant that Elle was getting used to him, and that he was going to stick around and be a part of their life. And that just wouldn't do, so "newest boyfriend" he remained.

Tall, dark, and handsome, Jerome had a talent for making Susan laugh. He seemed like a good guy, but Elle had seen the good guys come and go. As far as they were concerned, their mother's boy-friend was nothing but an awkward acquaintance eating cereal in a house that wasn't his. In contrast to Elle's hearty and healthy breakfast, Jerome was busy shoveling rainbow-colored sugar loops into his mouth. His diet was the worst Elle had ever seen, and they knew a lot of teenage boys. They'd never seen Jerome eat anything green unless it started with the words *sour apple*.

"Heya, Elle! Welcome to the waking world!" Jerome said with a smile.

"Mehmm" was all Elle bothered to muster in response. Jerome

looked back to Sue for support, who subtly gestured with her head toward Elle and mouthed the word "Go!" to her boyfriend.

"So, Elle, I, uhh—I was wondering if you had any plans this Saturday?"

Elle stopped mid-bite. Their eyes narrowed in suspicion. Was this some sort of trap? "If this is you trying to make me go to another football game, not happening. I did that *once* and it was just as bad as I—"

"Whoa, whoa, whoa, no need for the interrogation. I got no tricks or traps, promise." Jerome cut off Elle's tirade before it could start. "Just, you like *Phantom Thief*, right?"

The question caught Elle by surprise. "Umm, yeah. It's my favorite show. You know *Phantom Thief*?"

Jerome chuckled, showing off that effortlessly charming smile again. "Course I know *Phantom Thief*. That show's been running since before *I* was born. When I was a kid, they were on the Fifth Thief. He was this real suave British dude, like a James Bond with more funny catchphrases, and he'd use the phantom powers to walk through walls and he'd leave this card with a unicorn whenever he pulled a heist."

Elle jumped to their feet with a burst of fan-powered energy.

"Yes! He actually came back last year! It was called 'Unicorn in Captivity' and the Ninth Thief had to go through time to break the Fifth Thief out of space prison—it was the *best* part of the season!"

Jerome looked as excited as Elle. "No way! We gotta watch it later. I definitely need to see this."

Sue folded her arms and sighed affectionately.

"Oh God, you're *both* nerds. Watch out or I'm gonna shove you in lockers and give you wedgies."

Elle rolled their eyes. "Mom, *everyone's* a nerd now. It's weird when people *don't* like Star Wars or Lord of the Rings. And I just really like *Phantom Thief,* okay?" Saying they "really liked" the show was a wild understatement. *Phantom Thief* had changed Elle's life. Until a plucky, androgynous hacker became the Ninth Thief, Elle Campbell had never heard the word *nonbinary* before. They'd never known anyone who used they/them pronouns. They hadn't even known that was an option. They hadn't had the words to explain why everything in their life just felt *wrong.*

"The actor playing the new Thief, Nuri Something, they're nonbinary, right?" Jerome asked.

"Yeah . . . um—how did you know that?"

Jerome picked up a folded-up newspaper. "There's an article about them in the local paper. Bet ya didn't think the newspapers still had interesting stuff, huh?" He cleared his throat and read, "'Star of hit show *Phantom Thief* comes to town to promote their new graphic novel.'"

A lightning bolt of adrenaline ran down Elle's spine.

"What?! Where?! Oh my God, oh my God, oh my God. Nuri Grena is coming *here? This weekend?* How did I not hear about this?!"

Elle's thoughts were racing faster than their brain could process. Their personal hero was coming *here*. To their hometown!

Elle leaned over to read the newspaper article while simultaneously looking up info on their phone.

What's their book about? Elle thought. *How many copies should I get? Should I have it in advance or buy it there? Will they sign* Phantom Thief *merchandise? How many things should I bring for Nuri to sign? Should I confess that Nuri inspired me to come out? Or would that weird them out? What should I wear?*

To that last question at least, Elle instantly knew the answer: the jade dress they had been too scared to wear this morning.

"It's exciting, yeah?" Jerome said. "They're doing a bunch of signings all across town Saturday. So I was thinking that you and me could—" But Jerome was talking to air. Elle had already zoomed out of the kitchen, head buried in their phone.

"Taylor, what's up? It's Elle. I—yeah, I know I'm calling. Yeah, I *know* people don't call . . . well, *you're* weird! Well, maybe I don't *want* to text, ever think of that? Look, did you know *Nuri Grena* is doing a signing this weekend? *Yes* way, dude! They're coming to the bookstore on Powell Street. For real! I'm not messing with you, look it up! You think your dad could give us a ride tomorrow? Uh-huh . . . yeah? Awesome!"

Elle raced out the door, too excited to stay inside a moment longer. For the last six months, it had seemed to Elle like their life had been on pause. They'd somewhat retreated from the world to focus on figuring out the gender presentation that made them most comfortable. They'd quit all their sports teams, dropped out of the school play, and withdrawn from most everything except for being with their friends and watching *Phantom Thief.*

They liked to think of these last few months as their "cocoon time." But now they felt confident enough to go out into the world like a glorious genderqueer butterfly. And in a mere twenty-eight hours, Elle would meet Nuri Grena, the person responsible for changing everything. They bounced with delight, determined to start this new chapter in life by showing their hero the new, real Elle Campbell.

TWO

On a typical day, Elle trudged up the steps of the school bus with the weary resignation of a condemned prisoner. But today, nerdy fan excitement was coursing through them like rocket fuel. They didn't just walk up, they joyfully bounced from step to step.

When they reached the top, they were rewarded with the sour-faced expression of the bus driver. She directed Elle toward the back of the bus with a grunt and a jerk of her thumb like she was a baseball umpire calling a runner out. Elle flashed two thumbs up of their own and kept grinning. Nothing was bringing them down today.

Not even a withering glare from Casey Strick was going to dent Elle's spirits. On a normal morning, Elle would walk in dread of the icy-eyed tyrant of the seventh grade and her court of hangers-on. But today, Elle felt untouchable. They strode down the bus, a confident smirk on their face.

The smirk was quickly wiped off their face as the rickety bus careened down the road and sent Elle stumbling down the aisle. Elle was hurled from one row of seats to another like a human bumper car while the bus wheezed down the unsteady road. Eventually, they landed in an empty spot. Elle slumped over and put their head on their seatmate's shoulder.

"There, there, little flower. The mean ol' bus can't hurt you anymore," their friend Agatha Chen said. As usual, she wore all black save for the crimson-red frame of her glasses.

"This bus driver is totally trying to kill me," Elle grumbled.

"Probably!" Agatha responded with morbid cheer. "I personally assume that at least forty percent of the people I meet are plotting to kill me. And I *plan accordingly*." Agatha punctuated the final words with the knitting needles she held.

"Check it out," she said, holding up the fruits of her labor—half of a black scarf with a cutesy skull pattern decorating it.

"What if it had flowers?" Elle asked playfully. Agatha rolled her eyes. Their differing fashion tastes was a constant source of banter between them.

"You think *everything* should have flowers," she said with a pout.

"That's because everything *should* have flowers! Floral patterns are best patterns. Okay, compromise option. What if the skulls had flowers for eyes?"

"That was how I decorated the candy garden in the Willy Wonka play last semester, and now the drama club won't let me be in charge of props!" Agatha retorted with a huff.

"Speaking of, what time are you done with theater rehearsal tomorrow?" Elle asked. "Because, drum roll . . ." they started before Agatha interrupted them.

"Nuri Grena is doing a signing. I know. I overheard you *screaming* it at Taylor over the phone. Why couldn't you just text by, the way?"

"Maybe I didn't *want* to—no, I'm not doing this argument again," Elle said. "Where is Taylor anyway?"

"Napping." Agatha shrugged as she tended to another stitch of her scarf.

"Not napping," Elle heard from the row behind them. They

peered over to see Taylor Popopolis lying down across the bus seat, head resting on a backpack. Their town may have been hours away from the beach, but that wasn't going to stop Taylor from looking like a mini surfer dude in his oversized band T-shirt, cargo shorts, and shell necklace.

"I'm letting the energy of the universe flow through me to bring me in vibrational harmony with the day ahead," he said with a serene calmness.

"Totally napping," Agatha silently mouthed to Elle, who had to fight to contain their giggle.

"So yeah, I'm absolutely in for celebrity book signing. You may be the *Phantom Thief* megafan, but I've still got some comics for them to sign."

"Okay, but you *only* read the zombie alternate universe comics," Elle said with a sigh.

"Yeah, and they're *awesome!*" Agatha replied with the excitement of a shark that just smelled blood. Just thinking about the signing supercharged Elle's spirits.

"I'm actually going to meet *them*. Everything in life is like . . . there was *before* I saw Nuri Grena, and there was *after* I saw Nuri

Grena, ya know?" Elle wanted to show Nuri the confident enby they had inspired Elle to be, and thank the *Phantom Thief* star for all they'd done for them.

"I'm just amazed you didn't wear a full-on *Phantom Thief* cosplay to school today. A very admirable show of restraint." Taylor held up a hand with the pinky and thumb outstretched in the shaka sign as an extra show of friendliness. Elle was fairly certain that Taylor had never actually surfed, but somehow their friend had absorbed the surfer demeanor in its entirety.

"Well . . . if I'm being *completely* honest, that's more because I was already dressed when I found out about the signing and didn't have time to change," Elle confessed.

"Probably for the best," Agatha said while working on another stitch of her scarf.

"No offense, but Casey Strick would have had a *field day* if you showed up to class with an Ectoplasm Lockpick toy clipped to your belt." Elle rolled their eyes at the mention of Broderick Middle School's queen bee and stayed focused on the task at hand.

"Taylor, what time can your dad take us to the signing? I want to try to get there before a big line starts."

"He can't pick me up until after the basketball game tomorrow, so, like . . . eleven?" Tyler didn't do very well with a hard and fast schedule.

"This is *Nuri Grena*. We can't just *show up*. We need a game plan!"

Nuri was going to be appearing all over town for signings tomorrow, but which one should Elle try to catch them at? Taylor and Agatha wouldn't be free in time for Nuri's *Phantom Thief* trivia contest at a local restaurant, so that was out. And if Elle went to the signing at the art museum, they might get stuck looking at boring, stuffy paintings with their mother all day long. That left Nuri's appearances at the arcade and the bookstore. Elle imagined trying to have a conversation with Nuri at the arcade. Between the hordes of screaming gamers, the way-too-loud techno music, and constantly beeping video games, they would need to shout at the top of their lungs just for Nuri to hear them.

No, the best option to meet Nuri would be at the Purple Prose Bookshop. It was the actor's last signing of the day, but the bookstore was clean, quiet, and already Elle's favorite store in town. The perfect place to meet their hero.

"Okay, Nuri's at the bookstore from one thirty to four. Does that leave us enough time to get on line early?" Elle asked.

"*More* than enough time. It's gonna be all good. Don't worry, bro," Taylor said without thinking. He immediately realized his mistake, and his hands shot up to cover his mouth. The gendered term hung in the air like an awkward balloon before Taylor started stumbling over his own apology.

"Oops! I'm sorry! I didn't mean to call you—unless—I mean—are you good with bro? Or is it like a never thing? I'm sorry, I'll try—" Elle threw their hands up to cut Taylor off.

"It's . . . it's okay. Really." Elle knew people would make mistakes, even their friends. But it was always worse when people made too big a deal over apologizing and correcting themselves.

But also . . . well, sometimes they didn't mind being called "bro." Sometimes they didn't know which words they minded and which they didn't. It could shift day to day. It could shift person to person. Sometimes getting called a masculine term felt okay; sometimes it had the same effect as nails on a chalkboard.

Elle sat with their thoughts. How were they feeling today? Were they *actually* okay with "bro" today? Ell looked down at their cacti button-down and jeans. It wasn't *not* a bro look, they thought. More androgynous than feminine today.

But maybe the most important factor was that it was coming from Taylor. Taylor had been their friend before they had come out. They had been the only friend to truly stick around afterward. If there was anyone who saw past gender and just saw Elle for Elle, it was Taylor. Elle smiled. If it was coming from him, then at least for today, Elle was fine with being a bro.

"It's fine. I'm good being called bro right now. Just ask next time, okay?"

"You got it!" Taylor said, flashing a big grin and two thumbs up. Elle sat back in their seat with a satisfied smile. Still on the school bus, and they'd already gotten through the first gender-identity crisis of the day. They felt as invulnerable as Phantom Thief had in the episode where they wore an ugly Christmas sweater made of the Golden Fleece.

They could make it through anything today, so long as they knew that their chance to meet their hero was just on the other side of the sunrise.

THREE

The beginning of Elle's school day had moved at an agonizingly slow crawl. Math class had been a series of painfully cheesy pirate-themed word problems where Elle had had to "solve for X to find Captain Fraction Beard's buried treasure!" Music class hadn't been much better. The teacher had spent the entire period trying to make the class sing eighties power ballads. Elle didn't know what a Bon Jovi was, and they refused to find out.

Now it was time for gym. Elle stepped out of the bathroom into the hallway. They had traded their fashionable button-down for oversized gym shorts and an already dirty *Phantom Thief* T-shirt. Agatha was already there waiting for them. True to form, she had put together a gym ensemble consisting of all black clothes. Today was softball day. And while Elle would have preferred capture the flag or dodgeball, at least softball got them out of class and in the sun for an hour.

"Here, think this will get me out of having to do sports thing stuff today?" Agatha asked them, holding up a note of paper for Elle. Elle read the scribbled text on what was clearly a ripped-out sheet of notebook paper.

"'Dear Mrs. Gym Teacher, Agatha can't do gym class today because I diagnosed'—not spelled correctly, by the way—'her legs with . . . *jackedupitus*. Please prescribe'—again, not even close on the spelling—'her one day of sitting inside. Signed, Dr. Realdoctor.'" They looked at Agatha blankly, not sure what else there was to add.

"Okay, yeah. Not sure why I asked Taylor to write it," she replied, crumpling up the paper. Elle glanced at the clock on the wall and tried to count how many minutes until they were meeting Nuri Grena. They were so focused on the time, they didn't spy Casey Strick and her posse walking toward them down the hallway. Casey stopped and looked Elle over.

"Tsch, and you were doing *so good* with that *cute* button-down you were wearing. Totally something my *aunt* would wear. You just had to ruin it with a wrinkly old nerd shirt," Casey clucked at Elle. They looked at Casey and her minions, all wearing matching pink track pants and freshly ironed pink T-shirts. They looked down at their own outfit, and for the first time in their life felt underdressed for *gym class.*

"*Phantom Thief* is cool!" Elle protested.

"Look, I'm just looking out for you. They say if you don't consume different kinds of stories, you'll stunt your development. I'm only trying to *help*, Elle."

The mocking Elle could handle; it was that fake innocence Casey put on that really made Elle's blood boil.

"Well, what do you watch, then?" Elle replied, putting as much contempt into their voice as they could. Casey shrugged, refusing to be anything other than infuriatingly unflappable.

"Changes all the time. I'm kind of *cosmopolitan* like that. The big thing this week is British baking show judges reacting to jet ski fails."

Agatha leaned over and whispered in Elle's ear, "Hey, so I'm totally on your side, but those videos sound amazing and I'm absolutely gonna search for those links tonight." Elle lightly pushed their friend out of the way and kept their gaze fixed on Casey.

"I don't care what you think about me or *Phantom Thief*. I dress for *myself*, okay? Not for *anyone* else," Elle confidently declared.

"Trust me, that much is *very* clear." Casey's voice was as crisp and sharp as ice. Elle glared at her but struggled in silence, unable to find the right words to say. Casey and her friends turned and marched down the hallway, leaving Elle and Agatha in their wake.

"So that was . . ." Agatha said sympathetically.

"Yeah, I know. It was a solid comeback," Elle conceded.

"You had . . ."

"I had nothing."

"There, there, little flower." Agatha put her arm around Elle's shoulder. Casey had never bothered Elle before they came out. Maybe all those hoodies and oversized T-shirts had been an invisibility cloak that hid Elle from Casey's all-seeing eye for fashion. But ever since Elle started dressing the way they really wanted, it was like they had a target on their back that only the popular girl could see. She had never directly mocked Elle for being nonbinary, just for the things that made Elle feel happy being nonbinary.

"How did you stop her from making fun of *you?*" Elle asked Agatha. "She hasn't given you a hard time in a while."

"I just threatened to put a snake in her locker. Besides, all the things she thought were insults I took as compliments." Agatha looked up from her knitting to do her best imitation of Casey, nailing the popular girl's fake concern.

"*'Gee, Agatha, your clothes are so bleak and depressiony. I just want to let you know, so you don't feel bad, but everyone's saying they think you're creepy.'* Yeah, I'm aware! That's what the outfit is for. It's a specific vibe I'm going for and that vibe is *creepy!*"

Elle broke into giggles. They had always taken inspiration from Agatha's boldness. Agatha's determination to be herself had been a model for Elle when they first came out.

"Well, I'll figure something out," Elle declared, determined not to let Casey bring down their good mood.

"And if you don't, I've got you covered. Remember that scarf I'm working on?" Agatha asked. "What I'm thinking is that once I finish it, we sneak up on Casey from behind, you take the scarf, and you *squeeze* the—"

"Agatha—bad!" Elle barked at her. Sometimes managing

Agatha's more supervillain-esque tendencies felt like a part-time job. The friends shared a laugh as they made their way down the hall. When they stepped outside, Agatha trudged off to join the rest of the class at the baseball field. Elle stopped, and knelt down to tie their shoe. The autumn sun felt nice, and Elle was glad they got to spend at least part of the day outdoors. Their moment of quiet contentment was soon shattered, though, when they felt something heavy shove into their back.

Elle stumbled, then spun around to see who had knocked into them. Anger rushed through them when Elle turned to see the sneering face of Michael Pearman. He'd been a thorn in Elle's side for as long as they could remember. The two had butted heads since well before Elle came out as nonbinary, though that certainly hadn't helped. Elle didn't like to think of Pearman as a bully, but as a *nemesis*. The Constable Spectre to their Phantom Thief. Elle's body tensed; every instinct was screaming at them to charge and shove the boy right back.

But before they could do anything rash, Elle forced themself to take a deep breath and remembered a catchphrase from *Phantom Thief*: "An angry thief is a caught thief. Make plans, not mistakes." If they fought Pearman now, they could end up in more trouble than their rival. Before they could decide what to do, they felt another strong shove from behind.

This time, however, Elle didn't respond with rage, but laughter. Taylor had leapt onto Elle's back. They stumbled forward, but then their steps got more steady before turning into a full-on charge as Taylor pointed and steered them toward the baseball field.

"Onward, Elle-dorado! The field of dreams awaits us on this most spectacular of days!" The two made it to the grass of the field before Mrs. Samson, the PE teacher, blew her whistle and snapped at them.

"Popopolis, get off Campbell! No more messing around. This isn't time for games, it's softball!" Taylor hopped off Elle's back and the two made an unsuccessful attempt at stifling their laughter. Maybe gym class would be fine today, Elle thought, just as they caught sight of Michael Pearman swinging the metal bat. Even as a warm-up swing, Pearman whipped the bat around with a terrible force.

"What are you looking at?" he snarled. "Don't you need to go do your makeup? I know having your eye shadow right is *real impor-tant* for playing sports." Elle's fists clenched at Pearman's jeers. But they could be the bigger person. For today at least. They took a deep breaths and turned to walk away.

"It totally figures, though. You always looked like you *throw like a girl.*" The words cracked like a thunderclap. Elle couldn't tell which they were more offended by, the insult to their athleticism or the rank sexism. Anger overwhelmed them as they turned to face their nemesis. But they were startled out of their rage when a softball hit the chain-link fence that separated the two. The fence loudly rattled and shook; the softball had hit it with the force of a meteor strike.

"What's that about throwing like a girl, Pearman? Big talk for someone who went zero for three against Ruck Preparatory last week," Mrs. Samson called out from the pitcher's mound. Her arm was still extended from where she'd let go of the ball, a proud smile painted across her face. Pearman could do nothing but grit his teeth and scowl. Elle enjoyed watching Pearman stew in frustration, but the devious grin was wiped off their face when Mrs. Samson turned her attention toward them.

"Don't you go giggling, Campbell. He's right about your weak little baby throws. Plant your feet and rotate those hips!" Feeling slightly deflated, Elle sped off to take their position in the outfield.

The first batter stepped up to the plate, a large boy who Elle had never gotten to know very well, but who had always been friendly enough. Mrs. Samson stood on the pitcher's mound. She claimed to do it to make sure the game was fair for both teams, but her focused stance and her blazing-fast pitches made Elle wonder if the gym teacher was really just reliving old softball glories. The boy was up to the challenge, though. He swung smoothly and the bat connected with the ball with a mighty *thwack*. The ball sailed over Mrs. Samson's head and toward Agatha in the outfield. If she ran for it, Agatha could easily catch the ball.

"Chen, call it!" the PE teacher called out. Agatha's face scrunched up in confusion at the instruction.

"Uhh—here, ball? C'mon, that's a good ball. Come here," she said hesitantly. Her feet were firmly planted where she stood as the ball finally fell to the ground several yards in front of her. Even from all the way in the outfield, Elle could hear the sound of Mrs. Samson smacking her own forehead in frustration.

"Dang it, Chen! *Run* for the ball!" she bellowed as the batter jogged to second base. Agatha let out a bored sigh and started slowly walking to the ball.

"I said run! Gimme some hustle," said Mrs. Samson, annoyance rising in her voice.

"I *am* running!" Agatha protested, clearly very much walking. When she finally picked up the ball, the runner was rounding third and Mrs. Samson was all but begging Agatha to throw the softball. Instead, Agatha kept walking at her gingerly pace, ball in hand. She handed it to the baffled second baseman just as the runner crossed home plate. Mrs. Samson crossed her arms and looked ready to throw her glove in the dirt.

"Home run . . . I guess," the gym teacher finally said after letting out a long sigh.

Mike Pearman was next up to bat, and his attention was focused squarely on Elle. Elle gulped, then gathered their will, dug in their feet, and returned Pearman's fiery gaze back on him. The tall boy with the buzz cut took a few practice swings when he got to the plate. To Elle, it looked more like someone swinging an ax than playing a game.

Mrs. Samson turned back toward home plate. With a mighty windmill motion, she launched a fastball right down the middle.

Maybe they were imagining it—they were rather far from home plate, after all—but Elle could swear they could see a cold grin crawl across Pearman's face as the softball approached. He stepped forward, swung his bat around so fast Elle saw only a blur. Elle couldn't see the point of contact, but the loud thwack of metal bat against ball echoed through the field. Within a split second, it was clear that the ball was hurtling toward Elle.

Did Pearman hit it to them on purpose? Well, if that was how Pearman wanted to do this, then Elle was more than game. Elle imagined themself summoning a bolt of lightning to course through their body as their legs tensed and they took off like a shot. The ball was sailing overhead—all the way toward the edge of the field. Elle pumped their arms harder, willing their legs to pick up more and more speed. The ball was starting to fall, and there were still too many steps to go. Without time for a first thought, never mind second thoughts, Elle's feet left the ground. They were as airborne as the ball as they leapt toward it.

Elle stretched out their baseball-gloved hand as far as it could go. The ball was so close to the grass now, and Elle couldn't even see if they'd made it in time when their body hit the ground. Elle tumbled over themself in the grass, holding their baseball glove tight to their body. Elle looked down at their hand, and an ecstatic smile spread across their face as they saw the ball nestled in the edge of their baseball mitt. If their leap had been just two inches shorter, they never could have caught it. But they did. Elle took the ball in their other hand and triumphantly held it up in the air.

"Got it!" they yelled as loud as they could. They wanted to make sure Pearman heard them. The boy had just rounded second base when he stopped dead in his tracks, dumbfounded at the sight of Elle holding up the ball. He ripped off his helmet and slammed it into the ground before slinking back to the dugout.

"That's some great defense! Good hustle, Campbell!" Mrs. Samson proudly roared.

Elle smiled. Today was looking up.

FOUR

After a gym class of trials and tribulations, for the next few school periods, the worst Elle faced was boredom. The seconds ticked by slowly, but eventually they did deliver Elle to the final class of the day. The walls of the history classroom were plastered in dusty maps, and the door was guarded by a mannequin wearing the uniform of a Napoleonic soldier. Elle always eyed the mannequin soldier with suspicion. If their life ever turned into a real-life *Phantom Thief* episode, that mannequin had a 90 percent chance of coming to life and attacking.

Even though there was still forty-five minutes of school left, most of the class had already mentally left for the day. Some were staring intently at the clock, and others were struggling to keep their eyes open. The more artistically inclined students were whiling away the time with doodles in notebooks. Elle was spending their last precious moments before the teacher arrived engrossed in a *Phantom Thief* graphic novel they had brought from home.

"Ahem! Eyes up front! Your attention? It's *mine* now," called out a gruff, weathered voice that had all the warmth and charm of a growling rottweiler. Elle's head jerked up to see a wide, stout man with thin hair and a thick mustache carve his name into the chalkboard. The scowl on the man's face bore the weight of decades spent yelling at children.

MR. McMULLINS, the chalkboard read. A silent groan shuddered through the whole classroom. Up until a year ago, Mr. McMullins had been the most disliked teacher in all of Broderick Middle School. He had been infamous for his obnoxious distaste for any history that didn't involve, as he liked to call it, "the good ol' US of A." He had retired the year prior, but yet always seemed to still be hanging around the school.

Elle's mouth went dry; a substitute teacher was one of their worst fears. Their normal teachers all knew their correct name and pronouns. But a substitute? That was a different matter entirely. Would Mr. McMullins even understand what being nonbinary meant? Elle sank down in their seat. Maybe they could just hide and stay silent during attendance. Better to be marked absent than have to respond to a name that wasn't theirs.

But then Elle remembered how close they were to meeting their hero. Nuri Grena wouldn't hide from a challenge! Elle summoned their courage and stood up from their desk. They didn't have to rely on this substitute knowing their pronouns; Elle could walk right up and tell him. Elle was proud of themself for standing up for their identity. And it all might have gone well if the bell hadn't chosen that exact moment to finally emit its shrill, piercing ring.

"Class has started. In your seats!" the substitute barked to the class. Elle was already halfway to the front of the room, and tried to keep going. But when the substitute's basilisk gaze turned upon them, Elle froze in their tracks.

"I said to take your seat, young . . ." he started to say, but then struggled to find the right word to finish his sentence. Elle's attempt at androgyny had clearly worked. They tried to use the substitute's momentary confusion to get a word in.

"I just need to talk to you for one second. I want to make sure—"
The words tumbled out of their mouth as fast as they could talk,
but it wasn't fast enough. Before they could let the substitute know
their pronouns, McMullins silenced Elle with a stern wag of his
sausage-like finger.

"I don't care that I'm a substitute, there'll be *no* back talk in my
classroom! You hear me? Zero. Zip. *Nada!*" he venomously declared.
Elle opened their mouth one more time, but an impatient glare
from the teacher left the words caught in their throat. Defeated,
Elle trudged back to their desk all the way in the back of the class.
There was nothing they could do now but wait in dread. It wouldn't
take him very long to get through the As and Bs. Elle squirmed
with nerves as the substitute got closer and closer to Elle with
every name called out.

"Ellio—" the substitute started to say before Elle cut them off
as emphatically as they could. They didn't want to be called that
other name ever again.

"Elle!" they yelled, loud enough that the whole class suddenly
turned to stare at them. Elle swallowed a nervous gulp. No turning
back now. "I don't . . . I don't go by *that* name anymore. It's *not* my

name. My name is Elle. Okay?" Elle felt everyone's eyes on them as their words trailed off. Mr. McMullins folded his arms and threw Elle an annoyed look. Desperate to end the silence that hung over the classroom, Elle didn't know what to do other than to keep talking.

"And I also don't use he or she pronouns. It's they and them, those are my pronouns. Just want to make sure—"

"Well, that doesn't make *any* sense," the substitute teacher snapped. Elle flinched as the substitute teacher bitterly berated them.

"'They' describes multiple people. *You* are just one *singular* person with a head full of *nonsense*, and who's clearly in need of extra grammar homework."

Elle felt like they were being punched in the gut. They had explained their identity as plainly and politely as they could, just like they'd practiced with their mother. And it hadn't mattered. Mr. McMullins just . . . didn't care. Elle's sense of self and happiness simply did not register in the face of this man's absolute certainty in how the world should be. Elle opened their mouth, but they couldn't find a single word. But without any hesitation, Agatha suddenly leapt to Elle's defense.

"Excuse me, sir, but the singular 'they' pronoun has been in use since the fourteenth century! I can show you the web page from the *Oxford English Dictionary* if you want," Agatha said. Agatha's fake respectful tone made the impact of her unrelenting facts hit all the harder. Now that McMullins's "intellectual" argument had been demolished, he turned his scorn toward Agatha.

"No interrupting the teacher! If you want to talk, you can raise your hand," he hissed defensively. The face Agatha made in response was *technically* a smile, but all Elle could see was a face full of poison. Once the teacher's gaze moved elsewhere, Agatha turned her head to look back at Elle. Elle silently mouthed "Thank you" to their friend, and she made a heart shape with her hands in response. Elle managed a weak smile, but it was all they could do to hold back the tears prickling their eyes.

"Now, if we're *done* with interruptions, we can continue taking attendance," McMullins growled. Elle appreciated their friend's support, but it couldn't extinguish the hurt and anger churning in Elle's stomach. Having their identity so utterly dismissed, it made Elle feel like they shouldn't even exist. And now that the bad thoughts had started, Elle struggled to make them stop. How many other people at school felt just like Mr. McMullins did, but were simply not rude enough to say so?

Then I'll just find a way to convince them, Elle thought, determined to sweep away the darkness that clouded their mind.

They might not have the right words to make Mr. McMullins understand, but they knew somebody who surely would. And best of all, Elle was just one day away from meeting that somebody. Elle was certain that Nuri could teach them how to make people understand their nonbinary identity. This morning, Elle's goal had simply been to thank Nuri for all they'd done to help them. But now, it was clear that Elle wasn't done needing help.

That still left a whole day of feeling lost and hurt, though. They needed a quick escape, a little boost to carry them through the rest of class. Just then, Elle remembered the *Phantom Thief* comic book hiding in their backpack. Whenever they were feeling down, *Phantom Thief* had always been a comforting world that they could escape into.

When McMullins had his back turned, writing various dates on the whiteboard, Elle scooched down in their chair and tried to subtly reach for their backpack on the floor. With their eyes locked on the whiteboard, Elle carefully felt for the backpack zipper with their fingers. They opened the bag as slowly as possible, routinely stopping and scanning the room to make sure nobody had noticed them. Hands blindly searching inside the bag, Elle finally felt what they were looking for: the thick eight-pound history textbook and the much thinner softcover comic book. Smiling at their own deviousness, Elle slipped the comic into the middle of the textbook before pulling both books out of their backpack.

Elle cracked open the textbook, quickly turning the pages until they got to the part of the book they'd hid the graphic novel in. While McMullins droned on about how Joseph McCarthy had some good points actually, Elle was drifting off into the world of *Phantom Thief*. Within a few pages, they were completely immersed in the Ninth Thief's newest, most daring-est heist. With each twist and turn they absorbed, the pain of their argument with McMullins dulled. This was exactly what Elle needed; the book was a port in an emotional storm. A smile even started to crawl across their face.

WHACK!

Mr. McMullins slapped his hand against the top of Elle's desk. Elle jolted up in startled surprise.

"Glad we could merit a little of your attention. Mind contributing to the class?" he asked, eyebrows raised in condescending suspicion. Elle started furiously flipping through pages, trying to buy a few precious seconds to come up with something to say.

"I—um, um—I . . . uhh . . . was just looking for the right part of the textbook, so I could follow along. Get more detail on the . . . umm—the part of the chapter that we're talking about."

"And what part of the chapter would that be exactly? You know, since you've been paying such close attention," the substitute teacher replied.

"Uhh . . ." Elle got out, not even thinking thoughts, just making a noise. They scrambled to think of any kind of half-decent answer, but they ran out of time. McMullins took the textbook from Elle's hands. As soon as he lifted it up, the graphic novel fell out of the textbook and flopped against the floor. Elle was, in every sense of the word, busted.

McMullins picked up the comic book from the floor. He held it between his fingers far away from him in utter distaste. Elle couldn't tell if the look on his face was more disgust or astonishment.

"Okay, *Elle*. I'm gonna ask you this just *one* time. What is *this*?" the teacher hissed at them.

"Um, um . . ." Elle nervously stuttered in reply.

"Um, um, um—use your words! Were you, in *my* classroom, my place of *learning*, reading a *comic book*?" Mr. McMullins spat out.

Elle tried to think of an excuse, but their brain was shutting down from sheer terror. "Um . . ."

McMullins's eyes went wide with a flash of rage. "Say 'um' one more time. I *dare* you."

"Mr. McMullins, I'm *really* sorry," Elle began, putting on the pleading voice they usually saved for convincing their mother to buy them a new dress.

"Oh really? Are you *sorry*? Then you can write about how apologetic you are in *detention* tomorrow." The sentence handed down, McMullins turned to continue his class. But for Elle, it was like the earth had given way under their feet. They felt like they were in free fall. They couldn't be in detention tomorrow. They *couldn't*. They had to be at the signing tomorrow. This was it, their chance to meet *Nuri Grena*. They couldn't waste it locked in a classroom. Elle felt their breaths speed up and become shallow as panic raced through them.

"Mr. McMullins, *please*. I can't do Saturday. What if I do

detention *every day* next week? Or I could write a whole extra history essay? Just . . . just not *this* Saturday. *Please,*" Elle pleaded. A smug, satisfied smile crawled across McMullins's face. He sat down at his desk and kicked his feet up, one graded quiz crumpling slightly beneath his shoe heel.

"I don't know what world you think you're living in, but it ain't the real one. When you get in trouble, you *don't* get to negotiate. Something to think about when you're here bright and early tomorrow."

FIVE

On the drive to detention the next morning, Elle felt like they were being marched to the gallows. Their initial plan after getting detention had been to lie to their mother and face the consequences after the signing. But that admittedly shortsighted plan had gone up in flames the moment Elle got home. The school had already called Susan to inform her of Elle's punishment.

"You know, this wasn't how *I* planned on spending my Saturday either," Susan said, glancing at the rearview mirror to see a morose Elle staring out the window.

"Mhmm" was all Elle could muster.

"Had a whole day planned, and it did *not* involve dragging a mopey enby across town to school," Sue said. "Look, I know you were really looking forward to the signing, but you broke the rules, and actions have consequences. I don't want to be Mean Mom, and I know this isn't fun, but that's life, kiddo. And you know these actors are always coming to conventions and shows; there'll be another chance to meet Nuri Grena, I bet."

"Sure," Elle said flatly, too dismayed to utter more than one word at a time. It could be *years* before Grena appeared at a convention Elle could attend. And what would Elle do in the meantime? Who would show them how to stand up to the Caseys, the Pearmans, and the *McMullinses* of the world?

From the passenger seat, Jerome turned to face Elle, and silently mouthed "I'm sorry" to them. Elle slumped down in their seat and fiddled with the hem of their dress. That was the only part of this day that even remotely resembled a silver lining. With nobody at school on Saturday to see them, Elle could wear their favorite dress without fear of judgment or mockery. They'd gone all out with their outfit: constellation-pattern leggings, jade-green dress, comfortable red flats, and a silver necklace of a crescent moon. They'd even dared to put on a crimson eye shadow to match the red of their shoes.

Despite it being a Saturday morning, Broderick Middle School was a flurry of activity. Students with sky-blue basketball jerseys poured out of cars and into the school. An entire bus full of yellow-jersey-clad students did the same. Somewhere in the sea of basketball players was Taylor. Elle had forgotten there was a game being played this morning.

Elle also spotted theater kids hanging out outside the school entrance. Half of them were already in their costumes, and from the glittery wings and antler crowns, Elle wasn't sure if the department was doing a play about fairies or just reusing the costumes from last year's production of *A Midsummer Night's Dream*. Elle scanned the area to see if they could spot Agatha or Taylor, but had no luck finding their friends.

Elle pulled out their phone. They opened up the group chat the three of them had, and sent off a GIF of a gopher popping up from its burrow to ask "where u at?" Within a few seconds, Taylor and Agatha had both responded. Taylor's text was a string of emojis:

Elle had known Taylor long enough to know it was his way of

saying that he was already inside the gym for the basketball game, was sitting on the bench again, but whatever because now he could think about electromagnetism and outer space. Just a few seconds behind the emojis was Agatha's response, a giant wall of text written with perfect spelling and grammar.

It was a full rundown of the play rehearsal's status, layout of the prop room, review of various students' performances, and the latest gossip Agatha had overheard about theater drama. And there was *always* theater drama. Elle smiled weakly while reading their friends' replies. After a minute, Elle's phone buzzed in their hands— another message from Taylor.

U doin ok? the message read. Elle proceeded to shoot off a series of GIFs of characters either being sad in the rain or sad in a jail cell. The car lurched into a parking spot near the entrance. Agatha sent a GIF of a humanoid spider hugging a gremlin, in what Elle assumed was her way of being comforting.

"Phone down, kiddo. C'mon. I know this sucks, but time to get in there," Susan called from the front seat as she turned the car off. Elle let out a nondescript grumble and opened their door. Before Elle could step out, Susan turned around to face them with a look of sympathy.

"Elle . . . I'm sorry. I really am. Tomorrow, let's go out and we'll do something extra fun and special. How's that sound?"

Elle hopped out of the car. "Sure," they muttered. Their mother's sympathy felt bitter and hollow at that moment.

"We'll pick you up at two thirty. Try to have fun. *Love you!*" Susan called out through the window as she and Jerome drove away. Elle slung their backpack over their shoulder. They would have preferred to bring a purse, but the comics and snacks they'd need to make it to the end of detention required more space than a purse could provide. They'd packed a purse in the backpack just in case, so that made Elle feel better even if they knew that made no sense.

They looked up at the lumbering prison that was Broderick Middle School, and tried to steel themself for the detention ahead. They tried to take deep breaths, and made it to four when a loose basketball suddenly crashed into the side of Elle's head. Their temple stung, and any hope of calming down was lost. This was going to be the *worst* Saturday of Elle's life.

SIX

The cheeriness of the classroom they were condemned to felt like a personal attack. Prison walls of gold stars, smiley faces, and bubble letter math equations boxed them in. Elle looked out the window at the forest that lay beyond the parking lot, and let out a wistful sigh. They were the only one in the detention room that day, without even another student to share their sad fate with.

During a normal detention or boring class, Elle would kill time by coming up with a new *Phantom Thief* fanfic. One where the Phantom Thief came to a sleepy suburb town and needed help that only a snazzily dressed, nerdy seventh grader could provide.

But today, the thought of meeting Phantom Thief and getting to have a life-changing adventure felt like a cruel joke. Today was a real, *actual* chance to meet the Phantom Thief, or at least the actor who played them, and they were watching the opportunity slip through their fingers with every tick and tock of the clock. If this *were* a fanfic, Phantom Thief would burst through the classroom door, ready to whisk Elle away on an adventure just when they had given up hope.

The door did indeed swing open then, but it wasn't a nonbinary hacker from the future. Instead, a young, out-of-breath Black woman hurried in. Her heeled sandals were a fashionable shade of blue, but looked painful to move in. She had a big stack of papers in manila folders tucked under arm that threatened to spill out onto the floor at any moment. She could have secured the papers by holding them with both hands, but that would have meant looking away from her phone, which was apparently not an option.

"Sorry. Sorry I'm late. I got to the parking lot, but then I started watching a clip from *Bake-Off* and once you *start* watching *Bake-Off*, it's not like you can just *stop* watching *Bake-Off*," the woman explained in a single breath. She dropped her stack of papers on the teacher's desk in the room, and didn't pay attention to the several sheets of paper that fell to the floor. Elle recognized the young, motormouthed teacher, but only by reputation. Ms. Fambro had only started teaching at Broderick Middle School at the beginning of the year, and Elle had heard she was the kind of teacher who would give you full credit on a wrong answer so long as you made it a funny joke.

"Long story short, if I see one more grandma who doesn't know how to temper her chocolate, I'm gonna lose it," Ms. Fambro said, blowing a lock of hair out from in front of her face. Elle let a small grin break through the brick wall of their sadness. They were starting to get the feeling that this was detention for Ms. Fambro as much as it was for them.

"So . . . *detention*. Not how either of us wanted to spend a Saturday morning. Am I right?" she asked, slumping into the chair behind the desk. Elle nodded, and teacher and student let the conversation drift away into bored silence.

Elle bounced the tip of their pencil against an open notebook page, letting their thoughts drift off. They thought about what they'd be doing right now if they hadn't gotten detention. Fantasizing about it made them feel worse, but Elle couldn't help themself. They imagined being at the signing, standing at the front of the line. They would shake Nuri Grena's hand, and say something dazzling and witty. And then Nuri would have the most perfect advice ever. And then Nuri would come back and ask Elle to be their best friend, and they would fight evil lizard people together.

But there would be no meeting Nuri, no perfect advice, no making people use their pronouns, and no lizard people. Because they were stuck. Here. Alone. In Saturday detention. Ms. Fambro was spinning around in her chair and looking up at the ceiling, clearly as bored as Elle was. After only a few minutes, she declared that she was going for a snack break. Ms. Fambro brought back a candy bar for Elle, and by the time Elle had finished eating it, she'd gotten back up again for a bathroom break. They looked at the clock on the wall: only twenty minutes had passed since their mother had dropped them off at school. They let their head fall onto the desk. Even without the pain of missing the signing, this boredom would be unbearable.

Phones weren't allowed in detention, but with nobody else around, Elle couldn't help but take it from their bag. Their eyes stayed fixed on the door as they sent off a series of texts to their friends bemoaning their own boredom. Elle was waiting for the three floating dots to turn into words when Ms. Fambro walked back into the room. Elle didn't have time to put the phone away; it was in full, open view. The teacher stopped, looked at the phone, looked at Elle's scared face, and finally rolled her eyes and sighed.

"Whatever. Bad enough they're taking away your Saturday, least I can do is let you have your phone. 'Sides, I'm gonna feel all self-conscious spending all day on mine if you can't use yours."

Elle smiled and returned to their phone. At least now Elle could talk to their friends without having to stay on guard. Elle's focus shifted to social media, where despite promising themself a hundred times that they wouldn't do it, they found themself looking at Nuri Grena's newest posts.

The actor's feed was full of photos promoting the signing. Elle recognized several of the places around town that Nuri was posting from. There was Johnny Baseball's Hot Dogs & Home Runs, the combination restaurant and batting cages where Nuri would have their first signing; Hughes Park, the small park near downtown; and, of course, the Purple Prose Bookshop, where they would have their last signing of the day. Elle's spirits sank even lower. Nuri

Grena was *here*. In *their* town. Elle was so impossibly, infuriatingly close. And yet here they were—trapped in detention.

Elle sent the post at Johnny Baseball's to Agatha and Taylor, accompanied by a crying emoji. Hearts and hug icons came in response.

"Hey, would you be okay if I stepped out for a minute?" Ms. Fambro asked, rising from her chair. "I've got a date with my girlfriend tonight. I'm just gonna go outside and make a lil' video for her. That okay? You good here?"

Elle perked up when Ms. Fambro mentioned her girlfriend. Queerness would always get the young enby's attention. They couldn't recall ever having an openly queer teacher. Elle made a mental note to try to get a class with Fambro next year.

"Yeah! I mean—I'm good. Don't worry, you should go make that video for your girlfriend. That sounds totally romantic." It was the first thing Elle had said all day that wasn't a mope or a sigh. Ms. Fambro's face lit up with a smile. It occurred to Elle that maybe Ms. Fambro needed support for her queerness just as much as they did.

"Aww, aren't you a sweetie. Thank ya, love the dress by the way. Absolutely rocking that green color," she said with a smile as she made her way out the door, then suddenly poked her head back in.

"You're gonna stay here, right? You can watch videos or play games, but ya can't leave. Okay? I'm holding you to the honor system," she said sternly. Elle nodded in agreement, but apparently not convincingly enough, because Ms. Fambro needed extra reassurance.

"Pinky promise?" she asked, holding up her pinky finger. Elle held up their own pinky in solidarity.

"Pinky promise!" they declared. Having the room to themself was at least better than a teacher watching them all day. Even a fun, easily distracted teacher like Ms. Fambro. Elle immediately picked up their phone to inform Taylor and Agatha of their latest development.

Yo ms. Fambro just straight up left, they texted to the group alongside a laughing emoji. After a few moments, Agatha responded to the group text with a simple question that Elle had no real answer for.

Then what are you still doing there?

I can't leave, she could come back anytime.

And I made her a pinky promise!

It was too risky. And if their mom found out, she'd ground Elle until high school.

> Pinky promises are NOT legally binding.

Elle rolled their eyes; of course Agatha wouldn't care about lying to a teacher. But it was Taylor's surprisingly well spelled response that gave Elle pause.

> Had Dtention with fambro twice last month.
> She always leaves and doesnt come back till
> 20 minutes to end.'

Elle stared at their phone. They hadn't seriously considered escaping detention, but if Ms. Fambro really would be gone for *all* of detention . . .

U sure? they replied. Taylor responded with a GIF of a kitten nodding its head up and down.

Elle felt a prickle of hope. Could they really do it? Could they actually sneak out, make it to Nuri's early morning signing, and get back before the teacher noticed?

Jailbreak! Jailbreak! Jailbreak! came Agatha's enthusiastic response. Elle looked around the empty classroom. Breaking the rules was what had gotten them in trouble in the first place. Maybe it was safer to just learn their lesson and take their punishment.

Can y'all leave too? Don't want to go without you, Elle texted.

For sure. We've got a full-blown soap opera here. The actor playing the lead just found out his girlfriend is cheating on him with his understudy. Nobody's going to notice if I bail, came Agatha's response.

Think u can ditch 🏀 game? Elle asked Taylor.

DING

where will = way, Taylor wrote.

Elle scrolled over to check Nuri's social media. The actor had posted a new photo online—a photo of them in a glorious scarlet velvet suit outside the very bookstore Elle had spent so many Saturdays reading volumes of manga that they had no money to actually buy. Elle couldn't let this opportunity pass them by, not when the Phantom Thief themself was so close. First they'd need to escape the confines of Broderick Middle School, then make their way across town without their mother or anyone else they knew spotting them. The odds weren't on Elle's side. They knew it was more than likely they'd get caught, and end up in way more trouble.

But they had to try. They would happily take a month of detention over a lifetime of regret. They smirked and texted a single word to their friends.

> Jailbreak

SEVEN

The die was cast. Elle was going to escape this dreaded detention or get in massive trouble trying. Of course, now the immediate question was *how* they were going to do that exactly. The door to the classroom was unlocked, but between theater rehearsal, the basketball game, janitors, and teachers doing work, the school hallways were teeming with people who could spot Elle trying to flee. They couldn't very well stroll down the corridor and walk out the exit. Elle paced around the empty classroom. They always did their best thinking when they could walk around.

"Hmmm . . ." they said to empty air, deep in concentration as they moved through the rows of desks. Trying to come up with a plan, Elle thought back to various *Phantom Thief* episodes. There was a jailbreak episode every season; at least one of them had to have an escape plan that Elle could use. Granted Elle didn't have an Ectoplasma Lockpick on hand, so maybe the sci-fi show would be less useful than they hoped.

Elle made their way to the classroom door and cracked it open just enough to peek out. *Maybe* there was a chance they could just walk out without being seen? But that faint hope was dashed when a shadow started to round the hallway corner. Elle pulled their head back into the classroom. Clearly, they needed a better plan than "walk out the door and hope for the best." Fortunately, if there was one person Elle knew who always had a scheme up her sleeve, it was Agatha Chen.

Need an escape plan. Any ideas? Elle typed into the chat. Elle stared intently at the three dots that showed Agatha typing. After a minute, though, the dots disappeared. Maybe she was stumped too. Then Agatha's face filled their phone screen on a video call.

"Hiiii, little flower," Agatha's voice crackled over the phone. She smiled that devious smile that let Elle know a plan was very much in motion. Elle tried to figure out where Agatha was calling from. It was dark and dusty and they could see the room was full of shelves.

"Where are you?" Elle asked. Agatha turned the camera around, and Elle could now see the dusty and poorly organized prop room of Broderick Middle School's theater department. Crowns, fake swords, pirate hats, capes, and gowns crowded the shelves.

"Where am I? Oh, just at the location for *Phase One* of Agatha's super-awesome-devious-and-clever Detention Escape Plan!" she exclaimed with a dramatic flourish. For someone who wasn't an actor, Agatha certainly knew how to be theatrical.

"Is it safe to talk on the phone, though? What if someone hears us?" Elle whispered.

"Okay, first off, prop room is *way* out the way. You could totally commit a crime here, and nobody would notice," she answered.

"Honestly, I think someone already *has*," Agatha added. To illustrate her point, she grabbed a skull prop off a shelf and thrust it into the camera's view. "I mean, look at this. This is a *way* nicer prop than the other skulls. Like . . . *too* good," Agatha said with a worryingly joyful smile.

"Fair point. So what's the plan?" Elle asked

"Hold on, let me loop in Taylor. My plan is *awesome* and I don't want to explain it twice." Before Elle could respond, Taylor's face appeared on the screen beside Agatha's. His setting was the complete opposite of Agatha's. Rather than the closed, dark, quiet prop room, he was in the gym—open, bright, and crackling with the cheers of the crowd.

"Salutations, bro-migos!" Taylor yelled over the grunts, cheers, and squeaks of sneakers against court that accompanied any good basketball game. Elle smiled the tiniest bit; they felt better about Taylor calling them a bro if Agatha was a bro too.

"Gotten any playtime yet?" Elle asked.

Taylor's smile fell into an exaggerated frown, and he held up his fingers in a circle to represent a big ol' zero. "It is most unjust. Last game I was in, I made every shot I took," Taylor declared.

Agatha raised an eyebrow. "Didn't you accidentally score for the *other* team?"

"I still made the shot! Things like *defense* and *offense*—those are just a state of mind," he said with a confounding sense of confidence. Suddenly, Elle heard a sharp yelling voice from Taylor's side of the call.

"Popopolis! The *heck* are you doing?! Put the phone down!" the voice cried out. Taylor swung the camera around again—Elle was getting slightly nauseous from his nonstop camera movements— to view the mustachioed face of Coach Giardo scrunched up in a frustrated rage. While Mrs. Samson may have led the baseball team to victory and glory, he was an in-over-his-head math teacher who had gotten the coaching job mostly by virtue of having listed *Space Jam* as one of his favorite movies.

"I need you focused. Head in the game!" Giardo bellowed.

"Wait—why do you need me focused? Do you mean I'm gonna get to play?! I can do that! And I totally know which basket to shoot on this time!" Taylor rushed to get the words out as fast as he could. But Giardo only replied with an uncomfortably long silence.

"How about you go get the team some more Gatorade, yeah? Gotta keep the players hydrated," Coach Giardo eventually said. Elle couldn't see his face, but Elle could imagine Taylor's disappointed expression from the way his shoulders sank. They watched Taylor get up and jog out of the gym, the cheers of *"Here we go Bulldogs, let's go!"* getting fainter the farther Taylor got away from the basketball game.

"I'm sorry, seashell. I know you really wanted to play," Agatha began, putting on her most sympathetic face and using her affectionate nickname for the shell-necklace-wearing boy.

"But hey, silver lining! Now you can help with the escape plan, and we didn't even need to find an excuse for you to leave the game!" Taylor's face scrunched into a look of worried concern. "But what happens if I don't bring back Gatorade for the team?" he asked with the tone a puppy would if dogs could speak.

"They dehydrate and die? I dunno, man. Who cares?" Agatha replied with a shrug.

"Anyway, the mission at hand. Agatha, what's your plan?" Elle asked. They were starting to get antsy. If they didn't figure a way out soon, they might miss Nuri's first signing at the local batting cages. And if they missed the first signing, they would have to leave detention longer and travel farther. The longer they were out, the greater the risk of getting caught. Making it to the batting cages and rushing back was by far the safest option, but time was of the essence.

"It won't be enough to just escape the room," Elle continued. "We have to keep people from noticing I'm gone. There are janitors and teachers walking by all the time. If someone notices the detention room is empty, they'll call my mom, and then you just know she'll ambush me at the signing." Elle shuddered at the thought of making it all the way to Nuri Grena only to be snatched away right outside the door.

"Already figured that out," Agatha replied with a satisfied smile. "Everyone, meet the *fourth* member of our escape crew . . ." Agatha spun around a chair in the prop room to reveal a teenager-sized mannequin. The blank, lifeless face creeped Elle out, but Agatha was animated enough for both herself and the dummy.

"Unveiling their debut performance, I give you the Broderick Middle School Theater Mannequin in the once-in-a-lifetime role of Elle Campbell Decoy!" she exclaimed.

"Not to question the accuracy of our plastic compadre, Agatha, but that mannequin is pretty un-Elle-like," Taylor offered tentatively.

"*Pfft!* Sure, it may not look like Elle *now*. But trust in a little thing called movie magic. Or theater magic. Whatever kind of magic. Once we give Manny here a fashion glow up, it'll be just like the real Elle!"

"Ooh! I know just the thing," Agatha exclaimed in a flash of inspiration. She darted off the phone screen. And after a few seconds of noisy rummaging, Agatha reemerged with a prankster's smile, holding up a blindingly bright blue jacket with gold trim on the sleeves. Elle pouted and rolled their eyes. They knew *exactly* where this jacket had come from.

"It's from *Joseph and the Amazing Technicolor Dreamcoat*," Agatha said, beaming with pride. "Ya know, the story of a dude whose outfits were so obnoxious that his brothers threw him in a pit until he learned how to not dress like a Crayola box threw up," she continued with a malicious grin.

"Hardy har har," Elle retorted.

"Are you sure about that wig, though? My hair's not *that* long. I mean, not that long *yet*. Still growing it out. And is that from *The Little Mermaid*?" Elle asked while Agatha placed a flower crown atop a long, flowing wig of red hair.

"Eh, Ms. Sellers thought calling the character a *little* mermaid was sizeist, so it was more *The Healthy-For-Her-Body-Type Mermaid*," Agatha answered. Satisfied with the wig, Agatha stepped back to admire her work.

"It's *close*. We're almost there, I can feel it. It's like I'm looking at

Elle's twin, but it's still *missing* something," Agatha said, putting her hand to her chin in deep thought.

"Pants. The mannequin's not wearing any pants," Taylor pointed out.

"Yes! Good thinking, seashell!" Agatha exclaimed, diving back into the bowels of the prop room's seemingly infinite inventory.

"I thought of it because I usually forget to put on pants too. It's nice to have a reminder," he explained, beaming with pride.

A few seconds later, she reemerged, sporting an ear-to-ear grin and holding up a pair of sparkly gold pleather pants with purple stripes.

"Tell me these aren't the most Elle pants *ever*," Agatha squeaked, bouncing up and down with excitement. Taylor nodded in agreement. Elle just hoped that this meant the end of playing dress-up. The constant *tick tock* of the clock on the wall was making them painfully aware of how little time they had to pull off this escape.

"What about actually getting *out* of school, though?" Elle asked. "Once we get the decoy into the classroom, we still need to get me out without anyone seeing me. Maybe we could get a bunch of the theater costumes and tie them into a rope. Then I could climb out the window, what do you think?"

"Yeah . . . I, uhh . . . I'm not sure we should put *your life* in the hands of Ms. Seller's stitching," Agatha replied. To illustrate her point, she plucked a princess dress off a hanger and pulled. With little effort, the pink fabric ripped like tissue paper in Agatha's hands. "Plus the marching band is practicing out on that side of the school. They'd totally see you if you went out the window."

"No sweat, I figured out the perfect Secret Elle Transport Device," Taylor said eagerly. He'd moved into the locker room and was pointing his phone camera right at a large steel canvas basket on wheels filled to the brim with used basketball jerseys. Elle could swear they could smell the locker room through the phone.

"And the way you're gonna hide me is . . . behind the bin?" Elle asked hopefully.

"Nah, dude, we're gonna do it *sneaky-stealthy* style. You hop in, we hide you under the jerseys and wheel you right to the exit!" he explained with pride.

"So when you said *no* sweat, what you actually meant was *lots* of literal, *actual* sweat," Elle said.

"Yeah!" Taylor answered. Elle looked down at their dress. Their favorite jade dress. Elle always took super good care of it, made sure to never step in any puddles or eat their food messily when they were wearing it. And now they were going to take their favorite dress and submerge it in an ocean of tween stink.

"Mhmm, mhmm, not a bad plan. Not bad at all. Just, real quick, *one* suggestion. Instead of nasty gross jerseys, what if we filled the bin with nice, freshly laundered towels? Yeah? Operation Clean Towels? Who's in?" Elle suggested. Taylor grabbed a towel off one of the locker benches. He sniffed it, and immediately retched.

"I don't know about *clean* towels, but . . . uh . . . I'd stick with the jerseys, Elle-dorado," Taylor said. Elle watched with concerned confusion as Taylor took another big sniff of the towel, gagging once again.

"Yeah . . . definitely the jerseys."

"All right, let's do it," Elle said. "The mannequin and the jersey bin and the whole deal, I'm in. But if I end up stinking like a *gym sock* and Nuri Grena passes out from gross smell, I'm blaming *you.*"

EIGHT

Elle stared at the clock on the wall, watching the minutes tick by. With every moment that passed, Nuri Gena was getting closer and closer to their first signing. Every time Elle glanced at the door and Taylor and Agatha weren't there, more and more worry crept into their mind. What if something happened to them on the way over? What if the plan was derailed before it could even start? Elle stared down at their phone, simultaneously wanting for an update from their friends while also desperately hoping there were no unexpected updates to report. Suddenly, Elle could hear faint, muffled voices from outside the room.

"What are you . . . with that? Did you . . ." Elle moved closer to the door, putting their ear up right against the thin glass window.

Now they could make out the voice slightly better. It was an older man's voice, maybe a teacher or a janitor.

"I think that's supposed to stay in the drama room," Elle heard through the door. The pit in Elle's stomach grew larger. It *was* Agatha out there, and she'd been caught with the mannequin. Now Agatha would get in trouble just for trying to help Elle. The guilt of getting one of their best friends in trouble coursed through them. But then, Elle remembered one of Phantom Thief's catchphrases— something they said every time a heist was going wrong.

A great thief never lets their crew take the fall.

Elle's friend had come up with this escape plan all for them. The plan may not work, but there was no way Elle was going to let their friends get in trouble. They opened the door of the classroom, ready to stride out and take the blame for Agatha's mannequin theft. However, upon peeking their head out into the hallway, they realized that their intervention would be unnecessary.

"Shhh! You can't ask me that!" Agatha said forcefully. Elle peered out to see the back of a balding teacher, facing Agatha.

"I can ask you whatever I like, young missy. Now tell me what you're doing with that mannequin before I—"

"*Shh!*" Agatha cut the teacher off with another shush and a finger over her mouth for emphasis.

"Don't you know it's *bad luck* to say the M-word? Hmm! Do you want this play to be *cursed*?"

"It is? I didn't—I mean—but why—" the teacher stammered.

"Don't you know that this production is barely hanging on by a thread? We got more curses up in here than Macbeth opening King Tut's tomb! We need all the good theater magic we can get, and if that means dragging the lucky rhymes-with-shannequin around school to purge it of bad spirits and critics, then by golly I will *drag it!*" Agatha declared.

The teacher looked at the mannequin, then back to Agatha, then threw up his hands in defeat.

"Fine, whatever. Not dealing with Sellers and her nonsense," the teacher muttered as he walked away. Agatha smiled and flashed Elle a thumbs-up. The two had to stifle their laughter while they dragged the mannequin inside the classroom. It took them a while to arrange the plastic decoy in the desk. The knees didn't quite bend, and at one point an arm had popped off and needed to be reattached, but they eventually got it approximately in the seat. Elle paced the room, examining their stand-in from multiple angles, and came to the unnerving realization that the doll's eyes followed them across the room.

"This thing officially gives me the jeepers creepers, Agatha," Elle commented. They waved their hand in front of its face, half expecting the eyes to glow red and the plastic figure to come to life. It had happened plenty of times on *Phantom Thief*; the show usually did a killer-mannequin episode whenever they were trying to save on budget. "Are we sure this is gonna work?" Elle asked nervously.

"Just has to work long enough to get you out of school. Even if they realize, what can they do? Send a school bounty hunter to chase you down?"

"They can call my mom. And you know I won't get within a hundred feet of the batting cages or any of the signing locations if she knows I'm trying to sneak into the signing. Last time I got in trouble, she baked my phone into a Jell-O mold. Thing still smells like watermelon-cherry. So I—wait! What was that?" Elle's attention was suddenly grabbed by faint noises from out in the hallway. For a split second, Elle thought that maybe it was Taylor. But they didn't hear the squeaking of wheels from the jersey bin. And Taylor was more the "run full speed, then stop by crashing" type than someone who would walk steadily and calmly. Elle whipped their head around toward Agatha; her wide eyes and worried face mirrored Elle's own.

"Teacher," Elle silently mouthed. Without making a sound, Agatha pointed to the laminated world map that was pulled down over the whiteboard. Leaving the Elle decoy in the desk, the two raced to hide behind the map. The two just barely made it to their hiding spot in time when the sound of the turning doorknob froze them solid. Elle heard someone walk into the classroom, and realized too late that the map only covered them from the waist up. Their legs would be in full view to whoever it was who'd just walked into the room.

"Hey, Fambro, I'm going to get a latte. You want anything?" a woman's voice asked. Silence followed, and Elle and Agatha traded confused looks. Elle peeked out from the map just enough to see a young teacher standing near the door. The woman's face was buried in her phone, completely oblivious to her surroundings.

"Wait—did she leave her detention *again*? Oy vey, that girl's way too lazy for someone who doesn't have tenure," the teacher muttered to herself once she finally looked up from her phone.

"Okay, kid, trusting you to behave while Fambro's gone. Just stay here, do some work until detention's over," the teacher said carelessly. Now truly baffled, Elle peeked their head out again. The teacher was facing the mannequin, but her gaze was once again fixed entirely on her phone. "You're doing good, just a few more hours, then we can all get outta here," the teacher commented absent-mindedly as she walked out of the room, closing the door behind her.

A stunned Elle came out from behind the map, followed by Agatha, who was holding her sides and laughing uncontrollably. She looked to Elle, then to the mannequin, and started laughing even more.

"She thought *that* was *you*! Oh my God, these teachers are dumb. Told you this plan would work! " Elle approached the mannequin, and looked at it in its creepy, creepy eyes. "All right, Decoy Me, I guess you pass the test with flying colors. Don't let me down, I'm counting on you."

A rapid-fire series of knocks rapped against the door. There was no mystery to who was behind the door this time. Agatha opened it up to reveal Taylor, standing at the ready with the bin of jerseys.

"Your carriage of liberation awaits, Mx. Campbell," he said with a dramatic flourish. He looked over at the mannequin with its red wig, bright clothes, and flowers.

"So did the decoy work?" he asked.

"It totally worked," Agatha answered with a wide smile. Elle stepped out into the hallway to the bin of jerseys. Unfortunately, the smell was what they expected—an odious mix of old burlap and sweat. Elle wasn't sure they could bring themself to actually hide among the sweaty jerseys, but they tried to remind themself of the time Phantom Thief escaped from the Zoo Master's Menagerie of Madness by stowing away inside the pouch of a space kangaroo as a way to help psych themself up.

"Do either of you have any gum?" Elle asked their friends. Agatha reached into one of her skirt pockets—she insisted that all her skirts and dresses have pockets—and pulled out a packet of gum. Elle snatched the packet from Agatha's hand. They breathed its minty aroma in deep, and dumped every last stick of gum into the bin of jerseys.

Taylor leaned over and sniffed at the bin. "You know gum isn't gonna cover the smell, right?"

"It can't hurt!" Elle stepped into the bin, their friends helping submerge them within the basketball jerseys. Elle pinched their nose closed, and promised themself that a long, hot shower would most assuredly be in their future.

Once Taylor and Agatha were convinced that Elle was sufficiently hidden within the bin, they started wheeling it down the hall.

"The main entrance is too close to the gym, too many people there for the basketball game," Taylor pointed out.

"We'll head to the cafeteria instead. Take the exit out to the playground, then hop the fence to freedom," Agatha whispered.

The group made it down the first few hallways without incident. It was going so smoothly at first that Elle's heart finally started beating slower than a hummingbird's. The group moved cautiously, taking the time to peer around corners and check for students and teachers. They just had to sneak past the principal's office, ride down the elevator, then exit out the cafeteria to freedom.

"All clear. I don't see any of the phone ladies who live at the desks," Taylor said. Elle peeked their head out of the bin, and sure enough, this part of the school indeed looked completely abandoned. They let out a sigh of relief and leaned back in the bin. They were going to make it, they told themself, they were going to make it. Elle repeated it to themself like a comforting mantra.

However, their short-lived tranquility was shattered by the slamming sound of a door forcefully swinging open. Elle whipped their head around to see the school's janitor backing his cleaning cart out of an office and into the reception area.

Elle was struck with a bolt of fear, and the jersey bin ground to a sudden halt. Agatha and Taylor stood stunned and frozen. None of the daring detention escapees knew what to do. The janitor stared dumbfounded at the group. He looked like he needed a second to fully process the sight of a goth girl and a basketball player pushing school equipment through a deserted hallway.

"Hey! What are you kids doing with that cart? You ain't allowed to use that!" he shouted once he'd fully processed what he was seeing.

"What do we do? Agatha, you got a plan, right?!" asked a panicked Elle.

"Just one, and it's my *least favorite* thing in the world," Agatha replied.

"RUN!" she suddenly shouted. Agatha and Taylor kicked off the tile floor, and pushed the jersey bin as hard as they could. Soon they were picking up speed, and barreling away from the offices.

"You get back here!" roared the janitor as he chased after them in hot pursuit.

"There! Elevator!" Elle called out. With a burst of speed, Taylor sprinted ahead of the cart and slapped the button for the elevator to take them down. The doors slowly opened, and Taylor squeezed himself inside.

"C'mon, c'mon, c'mon," he cried, beckoning for Agatha to speed up.

Agatha struggled to steer the bin at these wild, breakneck speeds. Elle had to grip the sides of the cart to keep themselves steady while the bin swayed back and forth. The cart zipped through the elevator doors, and slammed into the back with a thunderous *wham*. For the first time during their escape, Elle was grateful for the pile of foul-smelling basketball jerseys and the padding they provided during the crash.

Taylor frantically pushed the button for the lower level over and over again. He stared at the still-open doors with a look of panic.

"They're not closing! Why aren't they closing?!" he bellowed. The janitor was charging at them like a raging bull. Like a lion chasing down his prey. And probably also some third kind of dangerous animal too.

Faster than they could even think, Elle sprang out of the jersey bin and slammed the "Doors Close" button with the palm of their hand. The doors lurched to life, and finally started to shut. For less than a moment, Elle and the janitor locked eyes. But before anyone could do anything, the doors sealed shut.

✿✿✿

After the elevator finished its descent, Agatha and Taylor steered the bin into the cafeteria. Elle poked their head out from their burrow of jerseys. They could feel how close they were now to making it out. A dozen rows of lunch tables were all that stood between them and the doors that would lead them outside. Elle breathed in, savoring this triumph. Most wouldn't enjoy the smell of gym sweat and cafeteria pizza, but to Elle, it was the smell of *freedom*.

"You think we have time to stop and grab snacks?" Taylor wondered, staring hungrily at the kitchen across the cafeteria.

"I'll go grab some. I know which drawer the lunch ladies and Lunch Todd keep the good chips in. You keep going with the bin, I'll meet you outside," Agatha said. She peeled away from the duo, heading to the kitchen and leaving Taylor and Elle to make the final stretch of the escape by themselves. They were so close to the exit that Elle almost dared to sit up, when a voice sent them diving back down below the jerseys.

"Well, if it isn't Mr. Taylor Popopolis. How 'bout you spin around and tell me why I'm seeing gym equipment in the cafeteria." The voice sent chills through Elle's body. It was the gravelly, self-satisfied voice of the man who had sent Elle to detention in the first place, the most dreaded history teacher to ever stalk the halls of Broderick Middle School: Mr. McMullins.

NINE

The teacher stood forebodingly above Taylor and the bin. Despite the fury radiating off McMullins, Taylor looked around the room before pointing at himself with innocent confusion.

"Me?" he asked, as though there was anyone else in the room that McMullins could have been speaking to.

"Yes, you," McMullins barked. The substitute teacher's voice echoed off the cavernous walls of the cafeteria.

"I'm not going to ask you again. Why am I seeing *basketball gear* being wheeled through the cafeteria?" McMullins barked. Taylor's eyes went wide from pretend confusion. He swiveled his head around, mouth agape.

"Wait, this is the *cafeteria*?! No wonder I couldn't find the basketball hoop!" Taylor said in mock confusion, running his hand through his blond curls.

"I must have taken a wrong turn at the art room. All those pretty finger paintings—so disorienting! I better get going. Thanks for the directions!" Taylor called out while attempting to wheel the bin back around to the cafeteria's entrance. Elle felt the bin come to a sudden, lurching stop as McMullins's voice froze Taylor. He put his foot out to block Taylor's path.

"Yeah, I don't think so. One more step and you can spend all next week in detention," McMullins threatened. Fear flooded Elle's mind. They couldn't get caught. Not now, not when they were so close.

"That equipment belongs to the school. You think it's yours to play with?" barked McMullins, cocking an eyebrow and folding his arms.

Taylor puts his hand on his chin, thinking for a moment before delivering his response. "Does anybody really *own* anything, though? These jerseys aren't just equipment, they're *experiences*. They belong to the seamstresses who made them, the players who wore them, the people who will, I hope, eventually wash them. So really, isn't it the *spirit of community* who owns the jerseys?"

The brick wall of smug stubbornness that was Mr. McMullins rolled his eyes at Taylor.

"No. School bought 'em, school owns 'em. That's called capitalism, kiddo. Now, I don't know what you're up to, but you ain't getting it by me," the history teacher promised as he strode past Taylor toward the bin Elle was hiding in.

"Umm, I, uh, uhh, I, umm . . ." Elle heard Taylor stammer. The boy's nervous desperation was palpable.

McMullins leaned over the bin and stared at the jerseys. Underneath the top layer of sweaty cloth, mere inches away, Elle was trying their best to curl up into a ball so small that they could disappear.

"Mr. McMullins, I was watching a video online, and they said that Thomas Jefferson and George Washington weren't actually *that great* of guys? Is that true?" Taylor asked, putting as much naive innocence into his voice as he could. McMullins snapped around, blazing fury in his eyes, any interest in the jersey bin momentarily forgotten.

"What?! Where you hearing that pack of lies? 'Cause let me tell you, those weren't just men, those were *titans of liberty*! You kids

87

with your PC nonsense think you can judge the men who gave you your freedom? I don't think so!" McMullins bellowed and raged. Taylor certainly had his full attention now, that was for sure. While the history teacher continued his rant on the failings of their generation, Elle poked their head out of their burrow of basketball jerseys like a gopher.

Elle quickly scanned their surroundings. McMullins's back was facing them; he was too occupied telling Taylor to go cross the Delaware himself if he thought he was such a big shot. Elle looked over toward the kitchen and saw Agatha standing on a sack of potatoes to reach the stove. Elle had no idea what Agatha could be planning, and hoped their friend wasn't escalating their crimes from detention escape to arson.

After turning on the burners, Agatha looked up and met Elle's gaze. The glow of the stove flame gave her grin a certain demonic quality.

"What are you doing?" Elle silently mouthed across the cavernous cafeteria. Elle didn't know if Agatha could understand them, but she did respond with finger guns and a wink. After that, Agatha disappeared deeper into the kitchen.

A moment later, Elle watched as their shadow-dressed friend dumped can after can after can of creamed corn into the largest pot she'd been able to lift up onto the potato sack stool. Agatha had set the stove burner to as high as it would go, and within a few moments the pot was starting to boil over. Agatha was like a witch tending to a cauldron of bubbling potion. She stirred her boiling brew until a thick, yellowish bubble of corn-flavored cream rose up, then burst in Agatha's face, splattering corn kernels across her glasses.

"And don't go playing armchair quarterback judge talking about how the founding fathers should have done *this* or *that*. Can't go putting *modern* values on men of history. Did they engage in some . . . historical practices that most would now condemn? *Sure.* But it was a different time, okay? Nobody was arguing it was wrong back then." McMullins droned on, consumed by his own tirade.

"What about John Laurens? He was around during those 'We don't wanna be England' times," Taylor replied. Mr. McMullins paused, and his eyes narrowed. There was no way Taylor would have learned about the eighteenth-century abolitionist from *his* class, that was for sure.

"How do you know about John Laurens?" he asked with a deep suspicion.

"Hip-hop musical."

McMullins shook his head dismissively. "Don't believe everything you hear, *especially* if it rhymes," he said. Taylor opened his mouth to respond, but McMullins cut him off with a wave of his hand. He turned around and started approaching the bin again.

"Enough of this. Don't think you're gonna make me forget this bin you're sneaking around with. Let's see just what it is you're hiding in this . . . What the . . . ?" McMullins voice trailed off as the sound of his steps suddenly went from the squeak of leather sole against tile to a wet *splorp.* The history teacher looked down to see a rapidly growing puddle of yellow, corn-filled sludge oozing across the cafeteria floor. McMullins darted his head to and fro in a panic, trying to find the source of the spill.

"No, no, no!" the substitute teacher yelled, speeding off in the direction of the creamed corn puddle's origin. He traced its path back to the kitchen, but he was so focused on the cream-slicked ground below that he never saw Agatha climb over the kitchen counter and into the cafeteria. She tiptoed around her boiled-over concoction to make her way back to Taylor and Elle. Elle popped up out of the bin, giving their friends a big grin and two thumbs up.

"Great work, y'all. That was awesome," Elle whispered as they carefully stepped out of the bin. They removed a jersey that was hanging over their shoulder, grateful to finally leave their sweat-stained hiding spot.

"You better not move, ya little punk!" they heard McMullins's irritated voice echo through the cafeteria. Taylor pointed to the doors leading out to the cafeteria. It was a straight shot, nobody who could spot them or stop them from escaping the school.

"Let's go!" Elle said strongly yet quietly. The three raced to the door. Caution was thrown to the wind; none of them even tried to hide the sound of their running. Taylor was the fastest of the three—his sneakers were easier to run in than Elle's flats, and Agatha wasn't moving fast no matter her footwear.

Reaching the doors first, Taylor flung them open for his friends. When the sun's light hit Elle's face, it was so much brighter than they remembered, and they thought to themself that the biting autumn wind had never felt so sweet.

TEN

Standing outside, taking in the fresh air and feeling the sunshine on their face, Elle wanted to yell out in joyous celebration. But they weren't in the clear just yet. Elle still had to cross the school parking lot before they'd secure their freedom.

"Let's move," they said to Taylor and Agatha in a hushed voice. The three friends crouched down, then started quickly shuffling across the pavement. Elle swiveled their head around back and forth, making sure no errant teacher or student was walking by. They were so busy checking for pedestrians, it never even occurred to them to make sure there was nobody still in the cars.

Elle walked around the front of a forest-green sedan desperately in need of a wash, and found themself face-to-face with Ms.

Fambro, the teacher who was supposed to be keeping them in detention.

Time slowed to a crawl, and the breath froze in Elle's lungs. As Elle helplessly stared at the teacher's unmoving expression, it felt like time was standing still. And then, after several more seconds of standing in front of the car, Elle realized time was moving normally. It was Ms. Fambro who was sitting still. She hadn't reacted at all to seeing Elle. Elle's fear gave way to confusion and curiosity. They peered closer into the car—her eyes weren't even open. The teacher had left detention so she could take a nap! She was too busy catching Z's to catch any runaway students.

Elle tiptoed away from the car, then broke out into a sprint as soon as they were far enough away. They caught up with Taylor and Agatha. The time for cautious sneaking was done; now it was a mad dash to freedom to the strip of forest that surrounded the school. The woods were like a portal. After a minute spent sprinting through branches and leaves, Elle had been transported from the school's parking lot to a cul-de-sac neighborhood. The sea of houses all looked like clones of the same two-story colonial architecture home.

Now that the school was out of sight, the three friends stopped on the sidewalk to catch their breaths. Elle sucked in gulps of air, holding their side and wincing. Not even the most strenuous gym class had inspired Elle to run so hard. As much as their leg muscles burned and their side stung with the pain of a runner's cramp, Elle had to admit that there had been something exhilarating about their frenzied escape. Elle didn't think they could run anymore, but at least they were still on their feet. That was more than they could say for Agatha, who had plopped down right on the neighborhood's sidewalk.

"No more running! Done! Done with running!" she called out in between frenzied gasps of air.

"I think we're good. Nobody chased us, and we're too far from the school now for anyone to spot us." Elle looked around the cul-de-sac and down the street. It was a lively neighborhood, plenty of people out and about enjoying one of the last Saturdays of the year before the cold winds would overwhelm the warm sun. There was nothing out of place or attention grabbing about three kids running out of the woods looking like they were playing.

The pain in their side started to subside, and Elle let out a sigh of relief. They still had a long way to go to reach the batting cages, but at least now they wouldn't have to be constantly looking over their shoulder.

"How you doing, spooky pants?" Elle called to Agatha. Agatha didn't lift her head or stop her heavy breathing, but she did raise a thumbs-up to affirm that she was, if nothing else, still alive. Elle next looked around for Taylor, hoping he was okay as well. But the boy was nowhere to be seen. Elle spun around, but couldn't see Taylor in any direction.

"Up here!" a voice called from above. Somehow in the forty seconds since they'd stopped running, Taylor had scrambled halfway up the branches of a tree.

"What are you doing? Why are you in a tree?" Elle asked.

"I dunno. Looked fun! I bet I can climb higher!" he responded excitedly, bouncing from branch to branch and sending orange and brown leaves tumbling to the ground.

"I can see the whole neighborhood from here!" he called out, excitement ringing in his voice.

"Do you see Johnny Baseball's?" Elle shouted up at him, trying to make themself heard all the way up in the branches. Taylor craned his neck, squinted his eyes, and looked around.

"No, not batting cages. Must still be too far, 'cause that giant hot dog it's got on the roof is hard to miss," he answered after a moment.

Agatha groaned in pained exasperation. "Ugh. I am *not* walking all the way to Johnny Baseball's. I'm serious. Someone carry me."

Elle pinched the bridge of their nose, trying to will a plan into their brain. It wouldn't be long until Nuri Grena was at the baseball-themed restaurant, signing autographs and leading a *Phantom Thief* trivia contest. But Nuri wouldn't be there for long. Elle tried to calculate how long it would take to walk to Johnny Baseball's, regardless of Agatha's complaints. If they had to huff it on foot, they might—*might*—get there in time for the very end of the trivia contest. But Elle didn't like their odds. And if they missed Nuri at the first signing, then the next signing location was even *farther* away. By then, if they had to walk, it would be physically impossible to both meet Nuri and make it back to school before detention was over.

Making it to Johnny Baseball's could be Elle's only real chance to meet their hero and avoid getting in more trouble. Plus the winner of the trivia contest supposedly would get an exclusive collectible statue—and Elle wanted that statue. Their best chance, likely their *only* chance, was to find some kind of vehicle. Bicycles would be perfect, but even something like skateboards or Rollerblades would help them travel faster.

"Maybe we call a rideshare? Just zip right to the signing," Agatha suggested.

Elle shook their head. "Can't do that. Rideshare apps are set up on our *parents'* cards. They get alerts for every ride we take. They'd know exactly what was up and where we were. Hey, Taylor! Let's get some recon while you're up there. Do you see any kind of vehicle? Anything with wheels?"

"Hmm, I got a lot of dads raking leaves. Lotta kids jumping in the leaves their dads rake. Big leaf culture in general. Ooh, I see one guy on a riding lawn mower. Does that help?" Taylor offered.

Elle tried to imagine the sight of them, three kids piled onto a lawn mower making its way down Main Street. "No, not quite what we're looking for," they responded.

"Okay, let's see . . . I see teens! Whole group of teenagers working on a car. We could ask them for a ride!" Taylor exclaimed excitedly. Elle appreciated Taylor's faith in people's goodness, but the idea of relying on older high schoolers for help was rather unappetizing. They looked over to Agatha, who was shaking her head emphatically.

"Nuh-uh! That's a *big* nope. I've listened to *too many* true crime podcasts, and half of them start with 'and then the victim got in the car with the mysterious teenagers she didn't know.' We get in that car, next thing you know they're finding our *heads* at the arcade and the *rest of us* at—"

"Okay, okay, we get the picture. The gruesome, awful picture," Elle said, cutting her off. They were starting to get anxious. Would they really have to walk the whole way?

"Hmm, vehicles, vehicles, vehicles . . . ooh! I see dogs! They're chasing that tennis ball *really* fast. Maybe we ride on the dogs?" Taylor suggested.

Elle and Agatha let their silence answer for them.

"Okay, yeah. Probably can't ride on top of dogs. But maybe we tie them to a sled and we *dog sled* to Johnny Baseball's?" he continued.

Agatha rolled her eyes. "Great plan! And just *where* exactly do we get the *sled* from?"

Taylor shrugged; that seemed like something the cosmos would provide for. "We could ask those little kids on the scooters. Maybe they have a sled!"

Elle's head jerked around—this could be exactly what they were searching for. "Hold on. Did you say scooters?" they asked Taylor. The pieces of the plan were starting to come together in their head. They would make that trivia contest yet!

"Yeah, about three houses down. They got this ramp, but it's only like six inches high. They are getting *no* airtime," he answered, mild disappointment ringing in his voice.

Elle turned toward Agatha and slyly grinned. "Let's go. I think I found our ride."

ELEVEN

"So what's the plan? We push them over and steal their scooters?" Agatha asked with a sadistic glee as they walked through the neighborhood, toward where Taylor had spotted the scooter-riding elementary schoolers.

"*Is* that the plan, Elle? 'Cause it'll work, but I feel like hitting kids is *definitely* how you earn bad karma," Taylor said, sounding worried.

Elle shook their head while continuing to stride down the street with confidence. "Don't be so dramatic, you two. We're not hitting anyone. They're just kids, it'll be easy. We'll ask to borrow their scooters, and then on the way back we'll get them a big bag of candy. Okay? Kids love candy."

They looked up and waved as the group approached the younger children riding their scooters in a driveway.

"Hey! How's it going?" Elle asked with as much friendly cheer as they could summon. The younger children stopped their scooters and stared at Elle and their friends with blank, stone-faced expressions. The girl wore a pink jacket, and pigtails jutted out beneath her helmet covered in rainbow and star stickers, while the boy had on both a sweatshirt and a helmet plastered with images of dinosaurs. Elle kept up their cheery demeanor, but was met with a wall of silence from the elementary schoolers. Now that Elle could see them clearly, they realized that the young boy looked familiar. "You're Lana Chansey's little brother, right? I'm Elle Campbell, I sit next to your sister in math class. How're you doing?"

The younger boy said nothing, then finally turned and whispered into his companion's ear. She nodded as he whispered to her, and glared at Elle sharply. "He says that you must be the weird one whose eye shadow is always too bright and is obsessed with *Phantom Thief*," she said in an accusatory tone.

Elle whipped around toward Agatha and Taylor with a concerned expression. "That's not really my reputation at school, is it?"

Elle whispered. Agatha and Taylor traded an awkward glance with each other, then reluctantly shrugged.

"It's not *not* your reputation," Taylor explained.

"*Anyway,* just wanted to talk with you real quick about these super-fun-looking scooters you've got here. What if you let us borrow them for the afternoon, and in return we bring you back a *giant* bag of candy?" Elle offered cheerfully. The little girl and boy stared into Elle's eyes so intensely, Elle felt like the children were peering into their very soul. If they started humming lullabies like the creepy twins in that horror movie Jerome had shown them, Elle felt they would completely lose it.

"You got the candy on you?" the girl said in a curt, no-nonsense tone.

"Er, well—not *on us* on us, but we'll stop by the store on the way back. Pinky promise! And we can totally afford to get you *lots* of candy too. Agatha sells gothy dog sweaters that she sews on Etsy, so we're talking, like, *eighteen* dollars' worth of candy. What d'ya say?"

This time, the boy wasted no time in whispering into the girl's ear. "No candy, no deal!" she barked at Elle. Elle turned back to face Agatha and Taylor. They threw up their hands. Elle's frustration was palpable. This negotiation was very much *not* going the way they had planned.

Every second they wasted arguing with elementary schoolers was a second they weren't traveling toward Nuri Grena. Elle didn't dare to check the time on their phone; they were afraid to find out just how little time they had before the first signing. They needed to get those scooters, and they needed to do it fast.

"Okay, so *now* we rob them, right? I'll push over the girl. You shove the boy, and then we grand theft scooter them," Agatha whispered excitedly while drawing Elle and Taylor in for a huddle.

"We can't push them over!" Taylor protested.

"Sure we can! We're bigger than they are. And they've got helmets on, they'll be fine," Agatha argued.

"No crime!" Elle scolded, sternly wagging their finger at her. They turned back around to face the children's icy demeanor. This time, they decided to be direct, no more friendliness.

"All right, cards on the table. You know what we want. Is there anything *you* want, or are we all wasting a perfectly good weekend?" If this was all business, they were going to treat it like business. The boy put his hand to his chin; Elle could see the mental gears were turning in the strange child's head.

"What should we do? Is there anything we want?" Elle heard the girl say softly to the little boy, who was still deep in thought. He responded with more inaudible whispers, and the girl's eyes went wide with shock. "Are . . . are you sure? That's, like . . . *a lot*. I'm not sure they'll go for it," she stammered nervously. But the boy nodded decisively, and that seemed to wipe away the girl's concern.

"You there, Green Dress," the girl said, pointing dramatically at Elle, "do you play *Battle Week*?"

"Umm . . . yeah. Why?"

"You play on the local servers. GhostCrook08, yeah? You play with the First Phantom Thief legendary skin, right?" she asked.

"No, no, no, no . . ." Elle nervously muttered, predicting where this was going. The *Phantom Thief* costume pack had come out last year, and the First Thief costume was now one of the rarest in the game. Elle had spent days and nights grinding and shooting and looting to unlock the ultra-rare skin.

"Whoa, *not cool*, little duderinos!" Taylor forcefully interjected.

"There is *no way* you're getting that costume. Elle worked really hard for it. *So many* side quests. What else can we get you?"

"If you want the scooters, then we want Phantom Thief!" she barked at Taylor. Taylor stepped back. He was out of his league against this four foot four enforcer. The little girl pointed at Elle and shouted, "Give us your skin!"

"Okay . . . Gonna need you to say that in a way that's a little less *serial killer-y.* Think you can do that?" Elle responded.

"I *liked* the serial killer way," Agatha whined.

The little girl scrunched up her face and balled her fists at Elle's demand for civility. Elle merely folded their arms and raised an eyebrow, unwilling to be intimidated. After a moment of staring each other down, Elle emerged the victor.

"*Fine.* Will you give us your First Thief skin in exchange for our scooters? *Please,*" the little girl grumbled.

"There, that wasn't so hard, was it?" Elle said, satisfied. Suddenly, they felt a tug on the back of their dress. They turned to see Agatha's worried expression. "Whoa, you're not seriously considering this, are you? You *love* that game skin. You use it *every* round. You don't have to do this, we'll find another way to the batting cages."

"It's okay, Agatha. Really. It's worth it to meet the *real* Phantom Thief," they whispered. Elle may not have expected to pay quite so steep a price, but it was a trade they were willing to make.

Elle faced the children, a content smile across their face. "All right, you creepy kiddos. You got a deal. You let us use those scooters, and I'll transfer you the game skin."

A smug smile spread across the little girl's face, and the little boy pumped his fist with excitement, then opened up the *Battle Week* app on his phone and handed it to Elle. Elle looked at the boy's gamer tag and scowled. They recognized the name; it was one that had beaten them many, many times before.

"There, it's yours. May your thievery be just and your pockets never empty." Elle recited the First Phantom Thief's catchphrase while handing the phone back to the boy, who clutched at his digital prize with awe. Not waiting for the precious tykes to alter the deal, Agatha rushed forward to grab the scooters.

"You have to bring it back by tonight," the little girl pouted. She crossed her arms and made a face while Agatha wheeled the scooter around her in circles.

"Yeah, yeah. We'll have them back by your bedtime. Now why

don't you run off on your little no-scooter-having legs," Agatha responded triumphantly.

"You know, there's *three* of you, but the deal was only for *two* scooters . . ." the little girl said with a malevolent grin.

"And I'm sure you of course just so happen to have a third one. What do you want for it?" Elle said with a sigh.

"You're a witch, right?" the girl asked, pointing up at Agatha.

Agatha stopped and almost beamed, clearly proud of the accusation. "I've been known to dabble in the works of Hecate from time to time," Agatha said, purring every word.

"I'll go steal my sister's scooter for you if you put a curse on a girl in my gymnastics class," the girl offered.

Agatha put her hand to her chin, considering it deeply. Elle shot her a look of tired bewilderment. "Do not cast a curse on a *child*, Ags." Elle didn't believe that witchcraft was real, but they didn't not believe in it hard enough to let Agatha go around placing hexes willy-nilly.

"Okay, okay. Compromise option. I can't cast a spell myself because . . . ugh, *morals*. But what I can do is . . ." Agatha knelt down to the little girl's height and pulled her phone out of her pocket.

"Okay, check this out. It's the *best* DIY voodoo doll channel. Follow the links, and you'll be banishing spirits under the waning moon in no time."

Happy with the deal, the girl skipped to the nearby garage, and came out a moment later with a rainbow sparkle scooter with a unicorn on the front.

"And you said dark magic would never solve anything," Agatha remarked to Elle with satisfied glee.

"I'd argue that was more the power of negotiation than dark forces," Elle said.

"Tom-*ay*-to, tom-*ah*-to," she replied with a shrug.

A few minutes later, Elle, Agatha, and Taylor were scootering past the entrance to the cul-de-sac. Taylor was in the lead, proudly riding the unicorn scooter in all its sparkly glory. Elle kicked off the pavement hard to catch up with him. The two traded a high five when Elle's scooter was even with Taylor's.

"Vehicles accomplished!" they triumphantly declared. Elle built up more speed, and felt the rush of the wind on their face. They looked up at the bright blue sky and let themself bask in excitement and relief. They were finally on their way! Elle was one step closer to meeting their hero. The thought of it fired Elle up. They were gonna get to that restaurant; win the *Phantom Thief* trivia contest because *obviously* they would; and make it back to school before Fambro finished napping, they promised to themself with a powerful determination.

And if they scootered fast enough, they could get to the restaurant before Nuri arrived, and still have time for one of Johnny Baseball's famous chili dogs! And Elle had every intention of moving fast.

TWELVE

Johnny Baseball's Hot Dogs & Home Runs had been on the corner
of Main Street for as long as Elle could remember. Many a birthday
party and Little League postgame celebration had been spent there
shoveling chili dogs into their faces. The decor of Johnny Baseball's
more than lived up to its name. Just to get in, you had to walk past
the eight-foot-tall statue of a baseball. On the inside, jerseys, pen-
nants, and posters covered every inch of the walls. Every TV screen
was tuned to a baseball game 24-7, and the games section was full
of old baseball arcade machines and baseball-themed pinball. Even
without the overwhelming stampede of baseball imagery, the batting cages ensured the restaurant section was still filled by the
constant melody of bat hitting ball.

Inside, Elle, Agatha, and Taylor found themselves sitting at one of the large tables painted to look like a vintage scoreboard and under a large banner that read W3LCOME FANTOME THIEF! Nuri hadn't arrived for their signing yet, so Elle had little to do but stew in anxiety and impatience. The restaurant was as busy as they'd expected it to be on a Saturday, but Agatha and Taylor had scouted it first to make sure nobody was there who would know Elle was supposed to be in detention.

As Taylor scarfed down his third chili dog, Elle carefully nibbled at their first. They were taking special care to make sure no chili spilled onto their dress; the last thing they wanted was to meet Nuri Grena with a big chili stain on their chest. Agatha, however, had lost interest entirely in the food. Her attention was completely focused on the trivia contest being led by Johnny Baseball's mascot, an unfortunate and underpaid teenager stuck inside a costume with a giant mustachioed baseball head.

To Elle, the questions about sports history might as well have been in a different language. For as much as they loved *playing* sports, *watching* them bored Elle to sleep. The *Phantom Thief* trivia that Nuri Grena would be hosting, though, now *that* would be their time to shine. Elle grinned, thinking to themself how impressed Nuri would be when Elle knew the really hard questions like "Which episode was secretly ghostwritten by the Prince of Wales?"

"Who can tell me the first and only MLB player to win All-Star and World Series MVP in the same year?" the mascot asked the room with his best impression of a game show host. Elle looked around; the other tables were full of families and friends, and a few were full of people in *Phantom Thief* gear, clearly also here for the signing. They thought back to when they were younger. How their mother would pick them up from Taylor's house after she got off work, and they'd come here to Johnny Baseball's every Friday night to celebrate the start of the weekend. And then during Little League season, she'd bring them to the batting cages when they wanted extra practice. Johnny Baseball's was even where Elle had come out as nonbinary to their mother.

They had been so nervous, Elle recalled. They'd spent the whole evening trying to steer the conversation toward the topic of gender, but it never came up naturally. So instead they'd just blurted it out when their mother asked if they wanted another soda. Elle had been so anxious and embarrassed, they'd shoved a fistful of cheese fries into their mouth so they couldn't say another word. It had been a dinner of deep questions, tough conversations, and lots and lots of hugs. Looking at the door, hoping to catch their hero walking through, Elle wasn't sure if they had been more nervous then or now. In the last half a year, they had grown their hair, gotten new clothes, and learned about makeup, but Elle still didn't know if they were missing something deeper about being nonbinary. What if they had just been focusing on surface-level stuff, and missed what was really important? For the thousandth time, Elle wished they knew another nonbinary person. Not just a character on the screen, but someone they could talk to and learn from. Elle didn't know if it was realistic, but they hoped Nuri could be that someone.

"Gonna ask that question again," the baseball-headed mascot said into his microphone. "Who was the only player to win both the—"

"LeBron James!" Agatha stood up on the bench and shouted, loud enough to match Johnny Baseball's voice coming out of the speakers. Her face was alight in mischievous glee.

"Let me remind the teams that you're supposed to *write down* your answers. Not *shout* them," Johnny Baseball responded with annoyance.

"And also, no. *Obviously* wrong," the mascot continued. The big foam baseball head may have had a permanent smile, but there was nothing cheery in his voice. Agatha sat back down at the table, grinning from ear to ear.

"Remember Mark Potter's birthday party when his dad got a trivia question wrong and totally flipped out?" Taylor reminisced while sprinkling a handful of french fries on top of his chili dog.

"I heard he grabbed a baseball bat and smashed a pinball machine," Agatha offered, still full of chaotic glee.

"He did!" Taylor said through a mouthful of french fry chili dog. Elle let out a sadness-tinged sigh. The pinball rampage may have been all anyone at school talked about the next week, but that's not what Elle remembered from that party. They remembered Mike Pearman's endless mockery. They remembered it being the first birthday party they had been invited to since coming out as nonbinary, and the baseball captain had done their best to make Elle feel unwelcome. For every trivia question Elle got wrong, every swing they missed at the batting cage, and every GAME OVER on the arcade machines, Pearman had been there with a cruel laugh and a biting comment.

Back then, Elle had been too scared about presenting as themself to do anything but silently absorb the mockery. At least now, while they still didn't know *what* to say, Elle felt strong enough to say *something* back. Even if it did get them in trouble for using "inappropriate language in a school setting" from time to time.

"Listen up, teams, next question!" Johnny Baseball's voice rang out over the loudspeaker, rousing Elle from their sorrowful memories. The half-man/half-baseball hybrid walked around the dining area, bouncing around to the delight of a toddler at another table.

"Who here knows which team started in New York, and later moved to San Francisco?" the mascot called out with a dramatic flourish. Elle watched as another mischievous grin snaked across Agatha's face. She leaned out into the row and yelled into the mascot's microphone.

"Megan Rapinoe!" squealed Agatha's voice over the loudspeaker. Johnny Baseball ripped the microphone away from her, and she collapsed back onto the bench in a fit of giggles.

"That's an official warning to Team Agatha's Christies! I'd give you a yellow card, but I'll get fired if I mention any other sports, so it's strike one," the mascot scolded. The angry voice coming from the smiley baseball face was such a humorous mismatch, even Elle and Taylor struggled to stifle laughs.

Elle looked around the baseball-themed restaurant. The decoration reminded them that for as much as they'd gained in coming out, they'd also given up some things too. Before coming out, Elle had always been on one team or another. Soccer, baseball, roller hockey; they had loved being a part of a team and giving it their very best. But since coming out, Elle had dedicated all their time to figuring out themself and all their new interests. They had needed that time, but now they found themself missing the thrill of sports.

"Hey . . . what would you say if I decided to try out for the baseball team next season?" Elle tentatively asked their friends. Taylor and Agatha traded unsure glances with each other.

"You, uhh . . . you think that's a good idea?" Taylor asked hesitantly. He shifted uneasily on the bench.

"It's just . . . it's not that you *can't*. You totally could. I mean—you're real good in gym class. It's just . . ."

"Pearman," Agatha interjected, finishing Taylor's sentence for him. Elle angrily sighed; it felt so wrong to them that a jerk like Mike Pearman could keep them from joining a team.

"I could still try out," they mumbled, crossing their arms and sulking.

"Could doesn't always mean *should*, Elle-dorado," Taylor said. To illustrate his point, Taylor lifted up his cheese-fry-loaded chili dog. "Like take this. I *could* eat this whole hot dog in one bite. But *should* I? Well, actually . . ." Taylor trailed off, his point forgotten as he opened his mouth wide and navigated the logistics of cramming the entire cheesy, chili-filled mess into his face.

"Say you make the team. You know Pearman would make your life miserable. And all his little baseball goons would make your life miserable too," Agatha said, jumping in where Taylor had left off. "It's not worth putting yourself through that. So just—sorry, hold on one moment." Agatha turned her head; something else had gotten her attention. She cupped her hands to her mouth and shouted as loud as she could:

"LeBron James!"

Elle hadn't even heard Johnny Baseball say the next trivia question, but they certainly caught the dirty looks the other tables were giving them. Johnny Baseball sternly wagged his finger at Agatha, who had the smug, coy smile of a house cat who had just knocked something breakable off the counter.

"This is your last warning, Agatha's Christies. One more answer that ain't baseball, and yer outta heres!" the mascot spat while making the hand signal an umpire would for a struck-out batter.

"I wonder, though, if you joined a team, which league would you play with? Would it be the boys' team or the girls' team? Ooh, or you could start an all-enby league!" Taylor said while wiping the cheese off his face with his hand.

Elle hesitated. It was a question they had spent long nights wrestling over. "I think . . . okay, first, this is, like, *just* for me and what I wanna do. It's all complicated, but . . . I think I'd prefer to still play with the boys. I definitely don't *feel* like a boy, but I still want to play against them, ya know? Ugh, it's all really confusing." They let out a defeated sigh.

"Look, maybe it's the theater kid in me talking, but do you really *have to* play sports?" Agatha asked. "I mean, you're trying to be more like Nuri Grena, right? Isn't their Phantom Thief super unathletic?"

Elle thought it over. Agatha was right about Nuri's Thief being clumsy and bad at things like fighting. The character's obliviousness to sports was even a running gag in recent seasons. But was that an individual quirk, or part of being nonbinary?

"So if the icon of all things nonbinary says you don't need sports, then maybe you're good?" Agatha suggested sympathetically.

Elle shook their head, frustration boiling up inside them. "But I *like* sports!" they exclaimed, bringing their fist down on the table.

"Maybe that's *their* way of being nonbinary, so . . . so maybe I have a *different* way of being nonbinary, yeah? I just . . . don't know what that way is yet." Hearing the words out loud made Elle even more disappointed that their hero couldn't be a perfect role model. Maybe if they knew a bunch of different nonbinary people, they'd feel okay with this, but they didn't. Nuri Grena was all they had, and not even that was right.

Elle felt the silence fall over the group's table. Taylor and Agatha squirmed in their seats, both of them unsure of what to say.

". . . Sorry," Elle mumbled, hoping to at least break the silence.

Agatha took Elle's hand and squeezed softly. "It's okay, little flower, nothing to apologize for. You're going through a whole big thing."

"And we're gonna be there for whatever you need, every step of the way," Taylor added. He also reached his hand out, but since it was covered in cheese, Elle opted to put a napkin in his hand instead. They smiled wistfully at their friends. Taylor and Agatha may not have fully understood what Elle was experiencing, but Elle still relied on their support.

"Which Major League pitcher holds the record for having pitched most career no-hitters?" Johnny Baseball called out over the loudspeaker, rousing the trio from their silence. Agatha turned to look at Elle with the pleading expression of a kid asking to open a birthday present the night before. "Go for it," Elle responded encouragingly.

Agatha's face lit up with chaotic delight. She turned around and yelled out to the mascot, "Ricky Vaughn!"

Elle didn't recognize the name, but Johnny Baseball seemed to from the way he put his hands on his hips and cocked his big giant, mustache-faced baseball head to the side. "That is a character from the 1989 film *Major League*! Which—okay, *deep cut*. Respect. But still not a real player! Yer disqualified! Get on outta here, Team Agatha's Christies," he berated them into his microphone.

"No regrets," Agatha said with satisfaction.

"No regrets," Taylor repeated as he threw the last handfuls of cheese fries into his open mouth. Elle wasn't paying attention to their friends, though. Once again, all their focus was on Nuri Grena. Or to be more accurate, the lack of Nuri Grena. An employee was busy setting up a signing area full of bottled water and *Phantom Thief*–logo-branded baseballs, but no Nuri yet.

"C'mon, c'mon . . . where are they?" Elle muttered while staring intently at the door, hoping to catch their hero the moment they arrived. But no matter how hard they glared, the doors to Johnny Baseball's stubbornly refused to open.

"Could you let me know when Nuri gets here? I wanna take some swings in the batting cage," Elle declared, and sprang up from their seat. Sitting and waiting was doing them no good at all. They needed to get up and move around before their head exploded.

And after the discouraging talk about sports, Elle was more than eager to prove their skills, if only to themself.

They made their way over the equipment counter, where the equipment manager was too occupied with a magazine to acknowledge Elle's existence.

"Can I get a bat and helmet for the batting cage?" Elle asked the burly, middle-aged man. He let out a barely audible grumble as he looked up from his magazine. Instead of meeting Elle's eyes, though, he looked down at their dress and let out an annoyed sigh.

"You sure you really wanna do that, little . . . umm . . . kid?" the manager asked. A flicker of warm pride sparked within Elle. Nothing gave them gender euphoria quite like a stranger reading them as completely androgynous.

"Yeah, I'm sure," they responded with pride and confidence. The manager took a long look at Elle, then finally shrugged and got up from his stool, slamming his magazine down as he walked to the back to grab the gear. Elle looked at the cover, and was more than a little confused to find a gorilla in shorts and a jersey dunking a basketball on the cover.

"Hey, uhh . . . what's happening on this magazine cover?" Elle asked.

"Don't you know? That's Barry B. Nanas. The first gorilla to play in the NBA!" the manager called from deep within the equipment locker. Elle had understood the individual words, but placed together they were nothing short of baffling. "That . . . *cannot* be real . . ."

"I'll tell you what's real, that gorilla's averaging fourteen rebounds a game!" the disgruntled equipment manager responded as he came back out with a helmet and bat. Elle took the equipment and turned away.

In the batting cage, Elle stared down at the pitching machine. They took a deep breath in, exhaled, and clapped their hands. It was a little psych-up ritual they had picked up from a lock-picking scene in an old episode of *Phantom Thief.* Before approaching the plate, Elle put on their helmet. To their surprise, though, their vision was obscured by a thick curtain of red hair over their eyes. It struck them then that they had never put on a batting helmet with their hair this long. They took the helmet off again, and brushed their hair back with their hands. Elle mentally kicked themself for forgetting to bring a hair tie, but eventually managed to get the helmet back on with only a few strands of hair still in front of their face.

Elle stepped up to the plate. They slung the bat over their shoulder and stepped forward to get into a batting stance. However, doing so made Elle's dress slide above their knee. Even though their leggings still covered everything, Elle still felt embarrassed by it. This was something they hadn't considered about playing in a dress. Elle shook their head, determined to banish the embarrassment. It was fine, they decided. If someone had a problem with Elle batting in a dress, then that was their problem, not Elle's.

Facing the pitching machine, Elle watched the yellow, dimpled ball roll into position, then shoot forward with lightning speed. They gritted their teeth, determined to hit the ball with everything they had. As the ball hurtled toward them, Elle stepped into it and started swinging the bat. But something was off; their swing felt slow. The dress was so much tighter around the shoulders than a shirt or jersey would have been. It was pushing back against Elle, and slowing their rotation. By the time they completed the swing, the yellow ball had already whizzed past them and crashed into the net.

Elle snarled in frustration. They were mad at not hitting the ball, mad at the dress for slowing them down, and mad at themself for being mad at their favorite dress. They redid their breath-and-clap ritual to recenter themself and calm down. Hitting the moving target that was their ideal mix of masculine and feminine was always going to be a challenge. They just needed to treat that first pitch like a learning experience. Now they knew that they would have to put extra power in their shoulders to compensate for the dress.

The next ball shot out of the pitching machine, its yellow dimples raced toward them. Elle was ready for it this time. This time, they rotated their shoulders extra hard and the metal bat whistled through the air. Elle kept their eye on the ball, and watched the bat connect with the tiny yellow comet. The loud *THUNK* of metal hitting hard rubber was music to Elle's ears. It was a cutting line drive that sailed right over the pitching machine. Elle felt triumphant when the ball slammed into the Astroturf on the other end of the batting cage.

The next pitch came—

CRACK

The ball was drilled hard into the net protecting the pitching machine. Pride surged within Elle. They didn't know exactly how to be nonbinary, but smacking a ball while having cat-eye makeup definitely felt right. Elle got back in position, ready for the next swing. The ball shot out of the pitching machine, and Elle started to swing when a voice called out:

"Elle! Elle! Elle!" Agatha exclaimed in a panicked tone as she ran up to the batting cage. Elle found their focus suddenly split between the ball and their friend. They jerked their head around to look at Agatha, and their swing spun them wildly out of control.

"Elle! We have to leave *right now!*".

"Gah! WTH, Agatha? Is it Nuri Grena? Are they here?!" Elle asked, excitement rising with every word. Agatha shook her head but was too out of breath to speak.

"P . . . Pe . . . Pe . . ." she sputtered between pants.

"Pearman!" blurted Taylor, who had suddenly sprinted up beside Agatha. Panic gripped Elle. If Mike Pearman saw them here, he wouldn't hesitate for one second to tell the school that Elle was cutting detention.

"We gotta go! Like, *right now*," Agatha ordered, having recovered enough to use words. "He and his goons just came through the front door." Elle dropped their helmet and bat onto the Astroturf-covered ground. This was a nightmare come to life for them. Agatha was right, they had to leave. But how could they when they were just *minutes* away from meeting the *Phantom Thief* star?

"But . . . but . . . Nuri . . ." Elle said desperately.

"I know, but you're not gonna get to meet them if you're too busy fighting Pearman. There's more signings today. We'll catch Nuri at the next one, okay? So shoo those Panic Goblins away, little flower," Agatha said reassuringly.

"But the next signing is so far away!" Elle protested, their brain too abuzz to think clearly. If they went to the next location, would they still have time to get back to detention before Ms. Fambro woke up?

"Then we'll scooter super fast!" Taylor replied.

Elle weighed their options. On the one hand, they didn't want to do anything that might jeopardize their chances of meeting Nuri. On the other, how could they have the perfect moment with their hero with *Pearman* standing nearby, mocking Elle's every move and writing tattletale emails to the school? "Okay, you're right. We have to avoid Pearman. We'll go to the next signing," Elle said, resigning themself to this change in plans.

"Great! I'll sneak into the equipment area. Maybe there's another jersey bin we can hide you in," Taylor suggested.

"No more bins!" Elle looked around frantically; they hadn't made it this far just to have the day ruined by their gym class bully.

Finally, Elle spotted what they were looking for.

"There," they said, pointing at a hallway behind the batting cages, "we'll use the employee entrance in the back."

"Right, so where *is* the next signing?" Taylor asked as they rounded the corner to the hallway. After looking over their shoulder to make sure nobody was following them, Elle showed Taylor the signing schedule on their phone. His face fell into a disappointed frown.

"Aww, man. Why do we gotta go *there*?" Taylor asked.

"Don't look at me, dude. I didn't make the schedule." They weren't thrilled about their next destination either. But if they wanted to meet Nuri Grena, they had no choice but to head to . . .

THIRTEEN

The M. Sara Museum of Art had always been a place that existed only in the magical realm of "field trip day." On an intellectual level, Elle knew that the museum existed year-round, but they had never even thought to visit on their own. And sure enough, neither had any of Elle's schoolmates. There wasn't a fellow student to be seen among the galleries of art.

Unfortunately, signs for Nuri's event were nowhere to be seen either. After scootering for nearly an hour just to reach the museum, the trio was now hopelessly lost among the twisting hallways and endless galleries. From the actor's latest social media post, Elle knew they were *somewhere* in the museum. But actually finding them was proving frustratingly difficult. Nobody browsing the museum on a Saturday looked to Elle like a *Phantom Thief* superfan. It was a motley mix of old folks, nerdy-looking couples out on dates, and at least four different men with tweed jackets and handlebar mustaches.

Elle, Agatha, and Taylor made their way through a hallway full of shadowy charcoals depicting distorted faces. Agatha and Taylor stretched out their faces to imitate the exaggerated expressions while Elle looked for clues to Nuri Grena's location. Their rapid footsteps on the hardwood floors echoed up the tall white walls. Elle was getting tired and frustrated by the maze of hallways—and they were pretty sure this was at least the second time they'd passed the same cubist mural.

Elle rounded a corner, and walked smack dab into Taylor. They had been so focused on their own worries, they hadn't noticed their friend come to a sudden stop in front of them. Elle looked up at the painting that had captured Taylor's attention. It was a large painting that was nearly the size of the whole wall—a splattering of pink and white paint against the greenery of plastic jungle leaves.

"What do you think it means?" Elle asked curiously. The painting was certainly striking, but Elle wasn't sure what to make of it other than wanting the shade of pink paint as a nail polish.

"Well, the green represents nature because . . . leaves and stuff. And how it endures the pink, which represents . . . I think it's cotton candy. Okay—yeah. It's a painting about how trees hate candy, but then also the white paint . . . which is clouds," Taylor said, offering his artistic analysis.

"I think it's about death," Agatha responded bluntly.

"You've said that about *every* painting we've looked at so far," Elle retorted with a roll of their eyes.

"And I've been right, like, three-quarters of the time!" Agatha said defiantly.

Elle smiled, then turned back to focus on the task at hand. They needed to find Nuri, and get back to school. The longer Elle was out, the greater the odds their escape would be discovered. And Elle didn't even want to think about if they missed Nuri at *another* signing location. Elle was so busy mentally yelling at Michael Pearman for making them miss the signing at Johnny Baseball's, they never heard the museum worker slink right up behind them.

"Ahem." She announced her presence with a cough. Elle

flinched and spun around. The museum worker was dressed in a black pencil skirt with a black blouse, sharp black glasses, and her black hair up in a bun. Elle thought that she looked like how Agatha might dress in twenty years. The trio hadn't been able to make a step without it echoing loudly through the museum, but somehow the woman had glided right up to them without so much as a whisper.

"The artist is communicating a very *specific* message with this piece. If you would be respectful enough to consult our written guide," the museum worker said in a huff, gesturing to a plaque on the wall packed with tiny text. Taylor started to read out loud.

"*Rue de Canal (1977)* was part of Jean Jeamont's series of mixed-medium paintings depicting the city life at the something something of the decade and speaking out against the bad thing that something-I-can't-pronounce wanted to do and . . ." he read, his voice trailing off as his focus waned. "Hey, museum lady, do we really have to read the whole thing?" The three of them turned around to face the museum worker, but somehow she had already disappeared, vanishing without a sound.

"Okay, I'll bet you both ten bucks that that lady's a ghost," Agatha said, looking around for the woman.

"Nah, no way. She's not a ghost," Taylor responded with a level of certainty that surprised Elle.

"Why? You don't think ghosts are real? 'Cause I can tell you some stories," Agatha said.

"No. It's because if she was a ghost she'd have left a trail of ectoplasm. Look at the floor—no ectoplasm!"

While their friends argued over the spectral status of the museum worker, Elle wandered off to look for her so they could ask for directions to the signing.

Elle continued through the galleries of the museum, looking for any sign of either the museum guide or Nuri. They rounded a corner and stopped dead in their tracks at the entrance to the next museum wing. It wasn't Nuri Grena, but what they found still left them spellbound. Instead of generic landscapes or indecipherable abstract art, this hallway was full of gigantic comic book pages and beautiful, intricate drawings of characters in striking poses and wildly inventive outfits.

"Wow . . ." Elle whispered to themself with wonder. Beyond the colors and clothes, what struck Elle so much was the androgyny the characters displayed. Every drawing showed a different person embodying both masculine and feminine qualities. Elle looked around in a daze. If they had any kind of internal queerdar like they'd read about on the internet, then all of this art screamed "nonbinary" at them. The comic pages depicted characters of all different body types, but Elle thought there was something both strong and beautiful about all of them.

"Are you a fan of the works of Kenichiro Ogata?" said the museum worker suddenly, her voice materializing out of thin air behind them. Elle was so startled by her sudden presence that they nearly jumped out of their boots.

"Eagh! You know, you are *really* good at sneaking up on people," Elle exclaimed.

The museum worker chose to ignore both Elle's comment, and their visible fear. "I'm not surprised it caught your eye. This exhibit has proven rather *popular* with the local youth," she said. Elle glanced at the museum worker with suspicious disbelief. It was hardly a mystery why this exhibit would be more fun than another hallway full of sunset paintings.

"Well, yeah—*obviously*. It's full of comics!" they replied with a self-assured tone. Given the choice between comics and not-comics, Elle would choose comic books every time.

The museum worker's face recoiled like she'd just smelled a rotten egg. "I'm sorry, but these are not mere *comics*. Mr. Ogata is a *mangaka*, a practitioner of the Japanese art of manga."

"Yeah, I've got the internet, Museum Lady. I know that manga is just the Japanese word for comics," Elle shot back, annoyed that they were being talked down to.

"This exhibit is dedicated to Mr. Ogata's seminal series, *BaBa's Eccentric Journey*. A little too *pop art* for my tastes, but I suppose if it's good enough to be displayed in the Louvre . . ." the museum worker continued with a sigh.

Elle marveled at a drawing taller than they were of a blond boy in a dazzling pink suit, with a piercing gaze, flowers in his long, wavy hair, and striking a pose like the ones Elle had seen in their mother's fashion magazines. These characters felt like they were calling out to Elle, just like Nuri Grena's version of Phantom Thief had when Elle first saw them. It occurred to Elle that if they hadn't discovered nonbinary identities through *Phantom Thief*, it might have been a comic like this that set them on their journey of gender discovery. Elle felt some comfort that there were more stories out there that made them feel seen as a nonbinary person.

As comforting as these fictional painted giants were, though, they had a *real-life* nonbinary hero to meet.

"Hey—I'm actually looking for the Nuri Grena signing. Could you show me which way it is?" But when Elle turned around, the woman had already vanished without a sound. Elle let out a disappointed sigh. Standing alone in the exhibit, among the drawings of stunning giants, Elle suddenly felt quite small.

They had to meet Nuri today. They *had* to. Because when it came to figuring out their identity, Elle didn't think they could take one more day of having to do it by themself.

FOURTEEN

Elle was still admiring the exhibit of hand-drawn manga panels when Taylor and Agatha bounded into the room.

"Little flower! There you are. I think we figured it out! Creepy museum worker, not a ghost," Agatha began, the words tumbling out her mouth at rapid-fire speed.

"Because of the ectoplasm," Taylor cut in to say.

"Right, because of the ectoplasm. But we're *not* ruling out that she isn't some kind of knowledge spirit," she said, visibly excited about her and Taylor's new theory.

"Probably an owl spirit, we think," Taylor replied matter-of-factly, like it was the most obvious observation in the world.

"Yeah—'cause she's all silent. Like an owl with those *stealth* feathers," Agatha said in excited agreement.

"Also her glasses just kinda *feel* owly, ya know?" Taylor concluded. Elle looked at their two friends, suddenly convinced that the pair had decided to share a single brain cell in the time since Elle had wandered off.

"What'd you find here, Elle-dorado?" Taylor joined Elle in looking up at the art.

"My new gender goals," they answered while doing their best to replicate the outlandish pose in one of the drawings. "What do you think? Could I pull it off?"

Agatha shrugged in response. "Look, if it's a choice between being stuck in an office and being what I'm pretty sure is a lipstick-wearing muscle vampire, I say follow your dreams."

After leaving the manga exhibit, Elle tried to stay focused on finding Nuri's signing. But as the group navigated the museum's hallways, they kept being sidetracked by the endless galleries of indecipherable art. The gallery dedicated to slices of bread in picture frames had been particularly distracting. Apparently *Pumpernickel in Oak Frame* was worth thirty thousand dollars somehow. Elle started to think that either they *really* didn't understand art, or that fine art was complete nonsense.

They checked the time. They couldn't believe how long they'd been wandering the museum with nothing to show for it. They needed to find the actor soon, before Nuri left for the next signing. There had to be a better strategy than walking around aimlessly, they thought. They jerked their head up when they heard Agatha's voice echo with excitement from around the corner.

"New best art!" Agatha shouted cheerfully. As they rounded the bend, Elle was transported from the white hallways of the museum to a room coated in sand and walls painted to look like a sunny day at the beach. The room was full of bathing-suit-wearing mannequins, all posed to look like they were doing normal beach activities like sunbathing, playing Frisbee, or eating ice cream. Elle immediately understood why this was Agatha's favorite. These weren't regular clothing-store mannequins like the one they'd dressed up earlier as Elle's decoy. No, this artificial beach was populated by about a dozen carefully posed plastic skeletons.

Agatha smiled gleefully and threw her arm around one of the skeleton's shoulders. "Tell me this isn't the best. I mean lookit this guy, he's wearing sunglasses! Why you wearing sunglasses, bud? You don't have eyeballs!" she jeered at her new skeleton friend.

They spotted Taylor staring with sadness at a skeleton of a dog, suspended in midair from a wire, forever reaching for a similarly suspended tennis ball. Elle could see tears welling up in his eyes, and they went over to comfort him.

"Hey now, no need for feeling the sads. That's how art wins. Look, it's all completely fake. Totally plastic. See? Like from a Halloween store. All the real doggies of the world are happy and doing awesome," they said soothingly, trying their best to reassure him.

"Well . . ." Agatha chimed in unhelpfully.

"*All* of the doggies are *fine*," Elle repeated with emphasis, staring daggers at an amused Agatha.

Taylor smiled softly and wiped the budding tears away from his eyes. "He just looks like such a good skeleton boy. I hope he gets the tennis ball," Taylor whispered.

"What do you think it all means?" Elle asked while examining a spatula-wielding skeleton placed in front of a grill and wearing an apron with BBQ BOSS written on it.

"Hmm . . . it's probably a commentary on mankind's obsession with entertainment and how our pursuit of distraction in the face of global crisis will lead to our destruction," Agatha answered thoughtfully. "So yeah. Consumerism, climate change, capitalism, yadda yadda yadda. Ya know, art stuff."

"You seriously got all that from this?" Taylor asked while staring at a snorkel-wearing skeleton building a sandcastle.

"Seems obvious to me." She shrugged in response. Elle stepped back; maybe they could understand Agatha's analysis if they saw the piece from a distance. Their focus fixed on the indoor beach, Elle didn't notice the museum guide until they walked backward right into her. Elle spun around in surprise. At least now they knew the mercurial museum worker had a physical body, more evidence against the ghost theory.

Elle sighed with relief. *Finally* they could get some directions in this topsy-turvy art palace.

"Oh! Hi, umm, we're, like—*really* lost. Could you please show us where the Nuri Grena signing is?" Elle asked, trying to sound as innocent and polite as they could.

"Please, keep your hands to the interactive sand portion of the exhibit! We ask you not to remove any of the models' costuming," the museum worker barked. Elle was taken aback by the sudden force in her voice, and it took them a second to realize that the models in question were in fact the plastic skeletons.

"Huh? We're not messing with the costumes. Right, guys—" they started to say, but stopped suddenly when they saw the sandcastle skeleton's snorkel gear had migrated over to Taylor's face.

"What costumes? I came in with this," he said innocently through the bright orange snorkel tube. The museum worker crossed her arms and glared at him intensely. Taylor pulled off the goggles and tried to put the snorkel gear back on the skeleton. He'd almost gotten it back on correctly when the skull fell off the body and landed in the sand with a soft thud.

"Sorry," Taylor mumbled bashfully, "I could fix that."

"I'd rather you didn't," the museum guide responded sharply. "This piece is titled *Head in the Sand* by modern art master Guillermo Lazlo de la Nadja," she continued, shifting back into her emotionless tour guide voice.

"Hey, Mrs. Museum, what's this represent?" Taylor asked, pointing at an ice cream cart manned by a skeleton holding an ice cream cone in each hand.

"The artist uses ice cream to explore the fragile beauty of the real. Every morning he sends a messenger who instructs us on what flavor to use based on the moods of a parakeet the artist befriended. Yesterday was Shrek Popsicles. Today the flavor is mint chocolate chip."

The three children all looked at one another with utter shock, then turned to the museum worker in horror.

"Wait—are you saying there's *real* ice cream in here?!" Taylor frantically asked. He immediately started circling the ice cream cart.

"Where are the spoons? Is there a scooper? Can I take this cone from the skeleton?" he asked breathlessly. Elle looked at the cart hungrily; there was *always* time for free ice cream.

"The ice cream is for *artistic display* only," the museum worker snapped.

"But it's *ice cream!*" Elle protested.

"It is *art*," she scolded. "It is meant to *illuminate the human condition*, not be *eaten*."

"Hold on, I think I know what's up," Agatha told her friends with a knowing smirk. She addressed the guide with a confident wink.

"You museum workers keep the ice cream for yourselves, then eat it once everyone's gone, right? I bet I'm right."

The guide bristled at the suggestion. "We are a staff of *professionals*, young lady. The cart is cleaned and the ice cream disposed of properly every evening," she spat at Agatha. Elle and Taylor stared at the museum worker, jaws hanging open in utter shock.

"I'm sorry, you just . . . *throw it away?!*" Taylor said in disbelief.

"That's so much worse. You get why that's worse, right? " Elle added.

"I assure you that I am much too busy and much too underpaid to concern myself with the judgment of children," the museum guide responded. Suddenly, though, her attention was snatched away by a short, squat, elderly woman with a messy poof of wavy white hair walking through the exhibit. Under each of her arms was one of the framed slices of bread from the other exhibit.

"Mrs. Gablogian, we've been over this. You can't use the art to make sandwiches!" the museum worker called out to the old woman. The guide scurried away after the absent-minded art thief, but somehow her hurried steps still didn't make a sound. The second that the museum worker left the skeleton beach room, Taylor turned to his friends with a fiery conviction

"So we're all agreed that we are *honor-bound* to steal and eat this ice cream, right?" he asked, looking at the ice cream cart hungrily. Agatha nodded in enthusiastic agreement. Elle was impatient to find the signing, but Taylor was already prying open the lid of the ice cream cart. Sure enough, inside were large three-gallon tubs of ice cream. Each one was bigger than Elle's head. Taylor looked into the bespeckled green circles of mint chocolate chip with awe.

The three friends descended upon the frozen treat, shoveling sporkful after sporkful of ice cream into their mouths—though perhaps Elle was a little more careful about doing so than their friends were.

As cold as the ice cream was, Elle felt warm inside. By all accounts, they should still have been in detention at that moment. Their legs should be getting sore from being crammed in the desk all day, and their eyes should be bleary from staring at a painfully slow moving clock. Instead they were surrounded by weird artwork, having fun with their best friends, eating forbidden ice cream, and soon—they were certain—they'd be meeting their hero. If this was wrong, it sure didn't feel like it. Elle helped themself to another sporkful, and it tasted like minty freedom with chocolate chunks of no regrets. Suddenly, out of the corner of their eye, Elle saw a tall, thin shadow approaching from around the corner.

"Museum lady is coming," they hissed to their friends in an anxious whisper. They knew it wasn't another visitor because Elle couldn't hear any footsteps squeaking on the hardwood floors outside the skeleton beach exhibit.

"Go, go, go!" they said, pointing toward the exit on the other side of the room. The three started sprinting toward the hallway, when Taylor came to a sudden stop halfway there. Elle whirled around to see why he had stopped running.

"What are you doing?" they asked frantically.

"The ice cream!" Taylor exclaimed in a panicked whisper. He turned back and raced toward the ice cream cart, the shadow on the wall looming larger with every footstep. Taylor managed to wrestle one of the ice cream tubs out of the cart, and started making his way back toward Elle and Agatha. But Taylor could only manage an awkward waddle while carrying it. It was too slow; at any moment the museum curator would come around the corner and catch him in the act.

"Roll it," they called out softly. Elle also made a rolling motion with their hands, just in case. Taylor wasn't the best at listening, but he was always killer at charades. Getting the message, Taylor put the unopened tub of ice cream down on the fake beach, and started rolling it quickly across the sand. He became like a tiny little steamroller, kicking up sand behind him and flattening a sandcastle with the ice cream tub. Elle grimaced when they saw that a pair of plastic scuttling crabs were in Taylor's path.

"Smash the crabs! Smash the crabs!" they heard Agatha chanting under her breath. Following the unheard command, Taylor charged right over the plastic crustaceans. It made a painful *crunch* sound that caused Elle to wince. It was at that moment, with Taylor mere feet away from the exhibit exit, that the museum worker marched back into the room. Anger was already painted across her face. She pointed at Elle and their friends and glared with a fury that truly did seem beyond this world. "You get back here! No more *tomfoolery* in the museum! You—you *art vandals!*"

The three middle schoolers raced away as quickly as they could.

They zigged and zagged through the hallways of art, trying to stay one step ahead of their pursuer. The trio had the slight advantage; they were sprinting while the museum curator was limiting herself to a brisk power walk. But that advantage would only last as long as they could keep running. Elle looked over their shoulder. They couldn't hear the museum guide following, but her shadow was a looming presence they couldn't escape from.

After scurrying into another exhibit full of statues, Agatha finally had to stop to catch her breath. Between this and fleeing the school, this was probably the most running Agatha had done in months.

"No . . . no more running. This . . . here . . . last stand . . ." she got out between pants of exhaustion.

"Last stand? What, like fight? I'm not fighting a grown-up! And if she is a knowledge spirit, she'd probably put some kind of *owl curse* on us or something," Elle responded.

Agatha, though, too busy gulping down deep breaths to get proper words out, shook her head vigorously. "No fight . . . just . . . just ice cream," she sputtered while lumbering over to the ice cream tub they had brought with them. Elle could still see the crab-shaped indent in the side of the container. Agatha dove into it spork first. Taylor soon joined her, and the two attacked the ice cream, trying to devour as much as they could before they were inevitably caught. After a few moments of ravenous eating, Agatha clutched her head in pain. "Ow ow ow ow!" she cried out, furiously rubbing her temples.

Elle sighed and shook their head in amusement. "Yeah, no kidding you got *brain freeze*, Ags. What did you think was gonna happen trying to *speed run* your way through three gallons of mint chocolate chip?"

Agatha shot Elle a dagger-like glare. "My lungs are *on fire*, but my head is *made of ice!*"

The ice cream and laughter was taking the sting out of not being able to find Nuri. Once the museum guide caught up to them, she'd surely kick them out of the museum. And Elle still didn't have a clue where the signing was supposed to be. They resigned themself to having to chase Nuri to the next signing. It wasn't what Elle was hoping for, but at least they still had more chances. They were knocked down, but not knocked out, they told themself. But the feeling of defeat must still have been written all across their face, because Taylor took one look at them, and he got back up on his feet and grabbed the ice cream.

"Nope! No defeat. We can still hide if we can climb up to the top of a dinosaur. She can't see us up there! Where's this museum's dinosaur room?!" he asked with an inspiring hopefulness.

Elle shook their head. Dashing Taylor's flights of fancy was never fun. "Sorry, buddy, they *don't have* dinosaurs. It's not that kind of museum."

Taylor's face collapsed. He looked like he'd just been told the Easter Bunny or Voltron weren't real. "What kind of museum doesn't have dinosaurs?!" Elle could only respond with an apologetic shrug. Suddenly, they felt a jabbing tap on their shoulder. Agatha was still in the throes of brain freeze, and was squeezing their head while poking at Elle.

"Rmmm!" she grunted through her intense headache.

Elle rolled their eyes; they didn't have a clue what Agatha was trying to say. "Words, Ags. Use your *words*," they teased.

"Grr!" Agatha growled in frustration, then quickly spun Elle around and pointed in across the hall.

"Mrr! Lkk!" She pointed at the sign on the distant wall. On it read the text PHANTOM THIEF SIGNING—THIS WAY. A wave of excitement and joy coursed through Elle. They had finally found Nuri's signing! They were gonna meet their hero! But then they remembered, they still had more pressing concerns to deal with.

"Get back here, you unruly, disrespectful, *destructive* children!" the quickly approaching museum guide ordered. It wasn't a yell, but somehow it was the loudest, most authoritative whisper Elle had ever heard.

"No worries, Elle-dorado. We've got your back," Taylor confidently declared. He picked up the ice cream container—evidently the trio had eaten enough to make it light enough to carry—and took off running to the gallery opposite of where Nuri's signing was.

"We'll distract the museum ghost, you get to the signing," Agatha told them, and followed Taylor down the hall. Elle nodded to her in confirmation, and split off from their friends. Elle darted into the next room, and watched the museum worker follow the melted green ice cream trail that Taylor and Agatha were leaving behind them. Elle held their breath in nervous anticipation until she was out of sight. Elle sprinted through the final hallway that separated them and Nuri Grena. They moved faster and faster, excitement building up with every step. They practically leapt into the room to find . . .

. . . a janitor cleaning up streamers and *Phantom Thief* posters, with Nuri Grena nowhere to be seen. Elle looked around the room in stunned horror. The space was utterly empty aside from Elle, the janitor, and the acrylic re-creations of James Webb Telescope photos that hung on the walls. They had *finally* found the signing. So where was the *Phantom Thief* star?

"You looking for the signing?" the janitor asked.

"Where . . . where . . . is Nuri?" Elle stammered, panic written all across their face.

The janitor took off his hat and rubbed his balding head. "Ai-yi-yi . . . I'm sorry, kid. That actor in the fancy suit just left 'bout five minutes ago," he sympathetically explained.

Elle felt like they had been punched in the gut. They sank to the floor and buried their head in their knees. Twice in a row, they had missed their chance to meet their hero. To learn how to be stronger as a nonbinary person. Elle knew there were more signings, but they'd already pushed their luck by leaving school for this long. Could they even make it to the next stop?

Elle looked at the cardboard cutout of Nuri. This may be the closest they would get to them, Elle glumly thought. Elle wanted to sit so still that they became a statue, and then get put on display in the museum so that nobody would ever argue with them about their identity again because their identity would be statue. But that wasn't really an option. No, there really were only two choices in front of them. They could either give up on meeting their hero and trudge back to school in defeat. Or they could venture on, risking trouble for another chance at glory.

Put like that, Elle certainly knew what choice the Phantom Thief would make. They looked back at the cardboard Nuri. The Phantom Thief was only beaten when they decided they were beaten. The fires of determination ignited within Elle again. The Phantom Thief would choose to move forward, and that's exactly what Elle was going to do too!

Elle marched back through the museum toward Agatha and Taylor with renewed energy. They soon strode into a room where the museum guide meticulously scanned the sculptures that crowded the exhibit room. They were a series of statues depicting people locked performing disco dance moves. Blue, yellow, green, pink—it was a series of pastel people forever doing the Hustle and Stayin' Alive. Anger sharpened the worker's features to a razor's edge. She slowly let out a breath, crossed her arms, and with a calmness that chilled Elle to the bone, started speaking to the two middle schoolers poorly hidden among the disco-dancing statues. "The now very *unwelcome* guests hiding in the exhibit, please consider this your invitation to *leave*."

Even though the museum curator was talking right at them, Taylor and Agatha didn't move an inch. "I don't think she doesn't see us," Taylor muttered as best he could without actually moving his mouth.

"Yes, I do see you," the museum worker replied bluntly. From their perch at the entrance to the room, Elle silently giggled watching their friends try to wriggle out of trouble.

"She's bluffing," Agatha whispered, stuck in a pose with one knee awkwardly bent and her index finger pointing to the sky.

The museum worker let out an impatient huff. She took off her glasses and calmly started cleaning them with a cloth. She wasn't even looking at them when she started speaking. "Here's what can happen. You can all leave *right now*, or I can stay right here in this room for the *rest of the day*. Just me and you. And you can stay in those *very comfortable-looking* dance poses all the way until the museum closes," the museum guide said with all the warmth of a hungry viper.

"And when I say 'all,' I do mean *all* of you. That goes for your friend behind me at the entryway too," she said, to Elle's surprise. They had no idea how she had even known they were there.

"Ya know what, that's fine. Whatever. My arms were getting too tired anyway," Agatha said, not hesitating to give in. The girl dropped her shoulders and shook out the stiffness in her limbs.

"Agatha!" Taylor exclaimed, looking visibly hurt. She rolled her eyes and brushed off his protest.

"It was my plan, seashell. I'm allowed to give up on it if I want to," she shot back at him.

"But we were *so close* to fooling the museum lady," he insisted.

"You really weren't," Elle responded, making their way back to their friends. The three trudged out from the statue exhibit. None of them were quite able to look the museum worker directly in the eye. As they all made their way to the exhibit's exit, though, Elle could feel her watchful, judgmental gaze following them. As soon as they stepped out into the museum hallway, Elle heard the guide call out to them. "And you are *banned* from this museum! You, and your children, and your children's children!"

Elle, Taylor, and Agatha traded confused glances with one another. Did being banned mean they could all get out of next year's museum field trip? Perhaps sensing that the punishment hadn't been as devastating as she had hoped, the worker quickly added:

". . . for three months."

Elle felt a thin smile creep up their face. They knew they should just keep walking, head out of the museum, and go to the next signing without making any more trouble. But Elle also knew they couldn't resist pushing their luck just one more time. Just a little bit. Just a teensy tiny little luck push. "Could we take the ice cream with us, though?"

All the rage returned to the museum guide's face in an instant.

"Out!"

FIFTEEN

When the Purple Prose Bookshop came into view, Elle felt their heart soar. It had been a long hour of scootering through town, and the trio had been forced to stop more than a few times to check the directions on Agatha's phone. On one occasion, Taylor's supposed "shortcut" nearly had the friends scooter right into the pond at Gillan Park. Elle had almost lost their scooter to an attacking goose, but Taylor distracted their aggressive avian assailant by throwing leftover french fries he had shoved in his pockets and yelling, "Smoke bomb!"

But one bridge, three shopping centers, and seven coffee shops later, Elle was finally rewarded with the familiar sight of the brick exterior and indigo awning of their beloved bookstore. The bookstore was Nuri's last signing of the day, but Elle had decided it was better to wait here than to try and rush to their signing at the arcade. This way, instead of another disappointing near-miss, Elle would be ready at the bookstore the moment the actor arrived.

The idea of *not* going to an arcade, however, was proving less than popular.

"Okay, but what if we *did* go to the arcade?" Taylor pleaded.

Elle shook their head. "No, no more running around chasing them. We're here. It's fine. We can wait. And it'd take us, like, ten minutes to get to the arcade from here. And who knows when Nuri's gonna end their signing."

"Nuh-uh! If we go down Hank's Hill, we can be there in *three* minutes. Less even!" he replied.

"Didn't you sprain your wrist last time you raced that hill?" Elle cocked an eyebrow and crossed their arms.

"Yeah—but that doesn't count. I was on Rollerblades then. Totally different situation," he said.

"Because scooters are *less* dangerous than Rollerblades?" Agatha asked.

"Yeah! Or maybe more dangerous, I dunno. Gotta be one of the two, though!" Taylor was hopping from one foot to the other, literally bouncing with energy. Elle stared at their friend, and intentionally let the silence hang for far too long.

"Okay," they finally began. "So the plan is to go *as fast* as we can down the danger hill, presumably break my leg, drag myself to the signing, somehow one-legged hop back to school and then . . . I don't even know at this point. Claim I got attacked by magic textbooks?"

"I mean, yeah, if you think it'll work!" Taylor said with an innocent grin.

"Okay, I don't vote for the big-hill-death plan, but I do vote for going to the arcade," Agatha said, wedging her way into the conversation.

Elle rolled their eyes. They knew what was motivating Agatha, and it wasn't meeting Nuri Grena or playing video games. "You're just saying that because you want to see Petunia."

At the mention of the name, Agatha's face turned a bright scarlet. She looked down at the ground, trying to hide the blushing and the bubbly smile that had snuck its way onto her face. "No! But . . . if she happened to be there, that might be cool . . ." she bashfully replied. Elle shook their head; they had made their decision. "C'mon, let's just get in line. I can already see people waiting outside," Elle called as they raced toward the bookstore.

"Ugh—there's already a line? Lines are dumb!" Agatha whined. Elle grinned slyly. Agatha might not have much patience, but this was *nothing* compared to the lines Elle had waited on in the past to indulge their *Phantom Thief* fandom. Two years ago at the comic convention in the city, Elle and their mother had waited through the night for the chance to get a photo with the actor who voiced Kibbles the Phantom Dog in the early 2000s. If they could endure eleven hours dressed as the tentacled Ptero-Monster from Planet Skull, they could handle a thirty-minute wait.

As Elle approached the Purple Prose, all their happy memories swirled together into an emotional smoothie in their mind. In first grade, getting to go to the bookstore was Susan's reward for when Elle did well on their math quizzes. In elementary school, Taylor's mom would drop the two of them off while she got her nails done across the street. They'd spent hours crouched in the corners among the rows of books, reading countless comic books they had no money to buy. Now that Elle was in middle school and earned enough allowance to actually shop at the store, they'd learned there was no better way to spend a cold and dreary Sunday afternoon than curled up in one of the big, velvety chairs in the store's café area, reading a good book and sipping hot chocolate.

Elle giddily bounced toward the bookshop like a rocket powered by rainbow sunshine. It felt like they weren't just walking toward a store, they were walking toward their *destiny*. But suddenly, Agatha darted out in front of them, arms stretched to block Elle's path.

"Stop!" she desperately ordered.

"The heck, Ags?! Get out the way!" Elle tried to walk around their friend, but Agatha refused to let them pass. Agatha put up her hands to protect herself from Elle's furious glare.

"Just hold on a second. Look over at the line, you see the girl over there? The one with the sparkly jacket and purple hair extensions," Agatha said, pointing at the group of people gathered outside the bookstore. Elle squinted and could indeed make out a tall girl who looked a few years older than them and matched Agatha's description. Elle wasn't sure where Agatha's apprehension was coming from, though. The prim girl in the pleated skirt wasn't doing anything other than waiting in line and taking selfies with her phone.

"Yeah, I see her. So what? What's the big deal? Please tell me this isn't some sort of weird goth girl vengeance grudge you got going on with her," Elle said.

"Nah, my goth girl vengeance grudge is against the wiccan priestess who works at the dentist. No, *that* is Kenny Shimura's older sister. Real influencer-wannabe type. I'm mutuals with her online. Girl posts, like, *twenty* times a day. Look, she *just* took another selfie. If you get on that line now, you *will* end up tagged in the background of a post. *Everyone* will know where you are before the signing even starts," she explained.

Elle's stomach sank. They were *so close* now. They could *see* where the signing would be, and still they had to hide and sneak. Elle vented their frustration by kicking a nearby pebble into the street. All they wanted was to talk to Nuri. Why did the universe keep throwing obstacle after obstacle in their way?

"Hey, so if Kenny's sister is so annoying, how come you keep following her?" Taylor asked curiously.

"Eh, she posts a lot of photos of her corgi wearing an astronaut costume," Agatha replied. Taylor and Elle nodded in agreement. Space dog content was indeed a very valid reason to follow someone online.

Elle looked back at the bookstore and let out a deep breath. "Okay, just gimme a second. Gotta gather my thoughts," Elle said, as much to themself as to their friends. They didn't want to spend more time on a wild-goose chase. Elle started to do the math in their head. If they left now, they should get to the arcade with a few minutes left in Nuri's signing. They'd have to get through the crowds, of course. And if the line was still long, the actor might leave before they got to the front. But, theoretically, if Elle was fast enough, they could still make it!

"Arcade. Arcade. Arcade," Agatha and Taylor whisper-chanted.

"Okay, we can go to the arcade," Elle said with a heavy sigh. It wasn't worth it to argue with their friends when they no longer had a better plan. "Worst case, we miss Nuri there and have to dash back here."

"And Agatha gets to see *Petunia*," Taylor teased.

Agatha looked down at the ground embarrassed. "I just never know what to say to her . . ."

Elle put a hand on her shoulder and tried to say something reassuring,

"Just look into whatever black void it is you call a heart, and I'm sure you'll find the words."

✿✿✿

As soon as Agatha set foot in the Bill & Duster's restaurant-slash-game-center, she made a beeline straight toward the object of her affection. She pressed her face as close as she could, and whispered, "Hello, Petunia, you shining hunk of gorgeousness. Are you ready to be mine?"

Suddenly, though, a shadow fell over Agatha, and she looked up to see the acne-ridden face of the high schooler behind the prize counter glaring down at her.

"Stop hitting on the scorpion statue!" he yelled. Agatha pulled her face away from the glass counter. On the other side sat Petunia, the twelve-pound gold-plated statue of a giant scorpion, golden stinger and claws as sharp as needles.

"Shut up, Roger! This is between me and Petunia!" Agatha spat. From a few yards away, Elle and Taylor watched the spectacle helplessly. Elle put their hand over their face to avoid attention, but watched Agatha's tirade through their fingers.

"Her name isn't Petunia, ya little brat," Roger argued back at Agatha. "It's *Scorpina*. Elegant yet deadly."

Agatha put her hands on the counter and jumped to raise herself up to even height with the high schooler. "That's a stupid name for stupid people! She's *clearly* a Petunia and you're gonna give her to me!"

"Oh, I will, will I? You got ten thousand tickets I don't see?" the arcade worker shot back at her. Agatha narrowed her eyes and focused her rageful gaze upon him, but did not in fact have ten thousand tickets.

"Yeah, that's what I thought."

Agatha slinked away, but refused to turn her back on the prize corner. Instead she kept her glare fixed on Roger and walked backward toward where Elle and Taylor were waiting.

"How have you not been banned from here?" Elle asked. The neon-pink lights of the arcade reflected off the lenses of Agatha's glasses. Together with her sharklike grin, she looked to Elle almost like a supervillain.

"I'm like the Moriarty to his Sherlock Holmes. He respects our rivalry too much to ban me," Agatha explained.

"You're crazy," Elle said with a chuckle.

"Crazy 'bout getting that scorpion statue! Now move aside. Mama's got tickets to win!" she boisterously declared. She and Taylor soon disappeared into the untamed wilderness of the arcade, and Elle continued their quest to find Nuri Grena. Bill & Duster'swas teeming with its regular weekend crowd. It was busy enough that nobody would spot Elle escaping detention, but also made it difficult to navigate. Blinking game lights, glowing screens, flashing sirens, and an ever-present neon-pink glow obscured any signs pointing to Nuri's signing. Even the carpet was loud, with its disorienting pattern of brightly colored squiggles and shapes.

Elle scanned the crowd, hoping to see other *Phantom Thief* fans who might point the way. But in a place like this, finding the nerds was like looking for a needle in a needle stack. *Everyone* was wearing a shirt from one franchise or another.

After they passed the same zombie shooter game twice now and were no closer to finding the signing, Elle started to get worried. They didn't have any time to waste.

Elle nearly walked straight into a *My Tiny Horsey*–themed

hunting game, but it forced them to stop and finally see the nearby sign pointing to Nuri. They followed the directions through the rows of games, growing more excited with every sign they passed. During their trek, they passed Agatha deeply engrossed in a round of *Ninja Ragnarok 7*. Elle hadn't played the game before, but they had watched a ninety-minute lore explainer video and all the ending cutscenes online.

Normally, Elle would be all about any game that let demon K-pop stars fist fight the Mighty Odin. But on days when Elle's feelings about gender were too complicated to handle—days like today—they tried to avoid games that forced them to choose between man or woman characters. Elle always hoped they'd one day find a game with real, human nonbinary characters. Too often their only options that weren't muscled-out action bros and bodacious battle bates were androids, aliens, or ghosts.

In too many stories they consumed, it was like people couldn't conceive of how someone could be neither boy nor girl unless they were an entirely different species. It was definitely better than no representation, Elle thought to themself, but it was tiring when it was the *only* representation.

That was part of what made Nuri Grena and their version of Phantom Thief so special. They were an actual human being who was nonbinary not because they were some kind of strange sci-fi being who didn't understand gender, but because it was what they felt inside and what they were happiest identifying as. Nuri had showed Elle that being nonbinary wasn't just real, it was deeply and wonderfully human.

Elle passed by Taylor plunking tokens into a Whac-A-Mole game. He looked excited as he gripped the watermelon-colored padded mallet, but his expression fell into a sorrowful frown when the smiling cartoon gophers started popping up out of their holes. Taylor stood at the machine, hammer raised, unable to bring it down.

"What's the matter, buddy? Can't whack the moles?" Elle asked. Taylor nodded, and Elle could see tears starting to form in his eyes.

"They're too *cute*, Elle. Just being happy little digging bros. They don't deserve to get malleted for that," he said ruefully.

Elle gave Taylor a reassuring pat on the back, and gently took the hammer from him. "I know, they're pretty cool. How 'bout a different game? Here, take some of my tokens. There's a game over there where you help a monkey climb a tree to get bananas."

Taylor's smile quickly returned, and he was soon back to his normal bouncy self.

"I'm gonna get that monkey *so many* bananas!" he exclaimed as he ran off.

Elle continued to the back of the arcade when a voice crackled over the loudspeaker. "Last call for autographs with Nuri Grena. Again, that's last call for autographs with Nuri Grena." Well, between the twenty-year-old speakers and the noise of the arcade, it actually sounded more like *"Lashcall fo agraph wi Nur Greno"*—but Elle had picked up enough to get the message.

Elle took off like a bolt toward the back of the arcade. This was exactly what they had wanted to avoid at the bookstore—a race against the clock to meet Nuri! After a few moments of sprinting and ducking through crowds, Elle came to a mass of people crowded around a signing table. This was *definitely* a *Phantom Thief* signing all right. The boisterous crowd was full of people wearing *Phantom Thief* T-shirts and costumes, and tightly clutching *Phantom Thief* comics, Blu-ray boxes, and posters. To Elle's frustration, the people in front of them were too tall for Elle to see to the front. Was Nuri still even here? They tried standing on their tiptoes and jumping, but they still couldn't see over the crowd.

Elle's heart was beating like a jackhammer. Was this it? Was this going to be the first time they saw their favorite actor in the whole wide world in person? They needed to get to higher ground. Looking around and thinking fast, Elle darted to a nearby racing game, and carefully stood up on top of the plastic motorcycle. It was difficult to balance, but when Elle looked up—there they were. Nuri Grena, waving and smiling behind the table, looking as radiant as the stars. Seeing their hero—even for just a flash of a moment, it took Elle's breath away. Apparently, though, standing on top of arcade equipment and being completely awestruck are rather difficult to do simultaneously. Elle started to wobble over after only a moment, and had to hop off the motorcycle before they fell off.

Once Elle got over the shock of having actually seen *the* Nuri Grena, they turned their attention back to the crowd. How would they even reach the actor? It was more of a signing *mob* than a signing *line*. And they didn't have much time; the announcer had already announced the last call for autographs before Nuri left for the bookstore.

As if to answer Elle's thoughts, the PA system screeched back to life. Thankfully it was much more audible now that Elle wasn't in the middle of the arcade jungle.

"We're wrapping up that signing, folks. But if you want *one last shot* to meet the Phantom Thief themself *and* win a bunch of exclusive merchandise, head over to the Lazer Cave! Make sure to register your team now. So get ready ladies, theydies, and gentle folks of all kinds, we've got lots of great prizes, but only one team can be victorious!" the mechanical voice announced. Elle jerked their head around, trying to make sense of what they'd just heard. Nobody seemed to know what was going on. Elle jumped up and down, and managed to catch a glimpse of Nuri . . . *leaving*?!

Where were they going? Elle was as confused as they were panicked. "What's going on?!" Elle heard someone yell from the crowd.

In response, an arcade worker stood up on the folding table that Nuri had been signing at, and shouted into a microphone. "What happened is y'all time travel thief nerds are a *pack of wild animals*! You can't form a line, you're yelling at the star, and some of ya stole the pizza from a birthday party! So we're gonna do a special competition, and the winner can meet Mx. Grena. And the rest of you can *get the heck out*!"

Elle quickly dashed away from the crowd. They needed to find Agatha and Taylor for their team. Elle grinned. Entering a crazy competition to win their prize was like a *Phantom Thief* adventure come to life. They were going to enter that laser tag challenge, and they were going to *win*.

SIXTEEN

To get through the crowd and nab one of the four precious team slots for laser tag, Elle had crawled through legs, climbed over arcade machines, and—while they weren't proud of it—had bitten a man in order to get at the Sharpie pen tied to the sign-up sheet. It hadn't been pretty, but they had accomplished their goal. Elle had managed to drag their friends away from their games, and now Elle, Taylor, and Agatha were now officially registered as blue team.

The laser tag waiting area looked like a rocky entrance to a cave hidden inside the neon-drenched arcade. Life-sized statues of an alien and a robot stood guard in front of fake boulders, and the wall around the cave had been painted to depict an epic sci-fi battle. Above the foreboding gateway were stamped the words LAZER CAVE.

Inside the fake cave was a hazy world of smoke machines, black light, and laser beams. Purple fluorescent bulbs cast an other-worldly pall over the players competing for a chance to meet Nuri. Elle could barely see Taylor's and Agatha's faces, but the white on his basketball jersey and the skulls on her dress glowed with a bright, brilliant light. Elle looked down at their nails; each of their fingers glowed a bright neon red from their nail polish.

Having to battle to meet Nuri, it was making Elle's heart race. If they lost, it would be another opportunity squandered. But as soon as the thought popped into their mind, they shook it out of their head. They couldn't think about losing before the match had even started. Elle summoned their courage, and their years of experience playing laser tag at birthday parties.

"Ready to win?!" Elle asked their friends, trying to psych them up for the laser battle ahead.

"Mmm, maybe. You think they'll let us use the lasers that are a bajillion degrees and cut people in half?" Agatha half-heartedly replied.

"Yeah, I'm hoping they'll stick to the *safe* lasers," Elle said, watching Taylor stare directly into one of the bright purple light strips.

"Safe? Did I just hear some *fool* call this Valhalla for the digital warrior a place of *safety*?!" a booming voice suddenly called out from the deep shadows of the hallway. Just then, a heavyset man in cargo shorts and a tactical vest stepped out to reveal himself. Under the black light, the lenses of his large sunglasses glowed a bright purple, and his beard and crew cut gave off an eye-searing orange light.

"'Cause listen here, sibling! There ain't no 'safe' in the LAZER CAVE!" the arcade manager bellowed in Elle's direction.

"Oh no, he's in character . . ." Agatha muttered under her breath. The disembodied purple lenses that were the man's eyes turned sharply in Agatha's direction.

"You want to see character? Then see what you're made of . . . *in the cave!* Find out if you got what it takes to survive *LAZERMANIA!*" the man's rumbling voice boomed through the laser tag waiting area.

"Is surviving Lazermania how we get the *Phantom Thief* statue?" Elle asked.

"You bet your keister it is! For you *elite few* who made it this far, we got a *special prize* today. The winning team is walking out of here with not just the *pride of victory*, but with . . . this!" Upon the final word, a screen in the corner of the room lit up. Looking at it, Elle gasped with shocked delight. On the television was a two-foot-tall statuette showing Nuri's Phantom Thief in their iconic green, black, and purple Krampus suit from the Christmas special where they robbed Santa's workshop. Elle's heart sped up with excitement. The collectible wasn't coming out for another five months, and was supposed to cost hundreds of dollars. Winning that statuette *and* meeting Nuri Grena would make this the official Best Saturday of All Time.

"Hey, could we exchange that boring whatever statue for a way cooler totally awesome golden scorpion at the prize counter?" Agatha said, raising her hand to ask the question.

"Ags!" Elle barked at their friend.

"What?! I wanted a statue at the arcade way before you did!" Agatha shot back at them.

"Stop right there, little warrior. You're talking straight *nonsense*. So clean out the earwax and get listening with your hearing holes.

There's only *one* rule in my domain," he declared. Suddenly, a pair of doors that looked like they were from a sci-fi spaceship started glowing blue on the opposite side of the cave, then slid open with a whooshing sound. Blue mist rolled out from the open doors and carpeted in the cave in a haze. The doors had opened to reveal a long hallway lined with laser guns and vests. For a moment, Elle wondered if they had actually been transported to a *Phantom Thief* starship. They were soon roused back to reality, though, by the arcade manager's growling voice.

"You want to *stay* in the Lazer Cave, you gotta *win* in the Lazer Cave."

"Now when I said one rule, what I actually meant was *lots* of rules!" the wannabe drill instructor shouted inside the laser tag hallway. Elle, Agatha, and Taylor were all sitting on a bench inside. Each of them had been equipped with a sci-fi-looking laser rifle attached by a cord to a clunky black vest. Elle noted that the vests they were wearing had blue lights prominently placed on the chest and back, to differentiate them from the other teams sitting in the waiting area.

The team in green-light vests were a group of kids who looked like they were Elle's age, though Elle didn't recognize any of them from school. Elle guessed they were simply another pack of middle schoolers looking for something fun to do on a Saturday. The yellow-light club were a cheery team of adult-age *Phantom Thief* fans. But the red-light team . . . the red-light team was a different matter entirely. They didn't look like they were there to meet an actor, they looked like they were there to wage laser *war*.

Aside from the glowing red bulbs on their vests, all four of them were dressed head to toe in black. Black shoes, black pants, black sweatshirts, black gloves. They even all had black bandannas over their faces and wore black backward baseball hats. Elle couldn't make out the boys' faces, but from their heights alone Elle could guess they were in high school. Seventeen at the youngest, Elle thought to themself.

Elle's first thought was how organized and cool the older boys looked. They looked like the kind of sci-fi ninja henchmen who would attack Phantom Thief. Elle's second thought, though, was how lame it was to be taking *laser tag* of all things so seriously at that age. Elle didn't plan on growing out of their own childhood hobbies, but, like . . . c'mon. At least be proper teenage dirtbags and graduate to paintball. Not to mention it seemed like a lose-lose scenario. Either they were the jerks who beat up on kids at a party game, or they were the teens who got their butts kicked by a bunch of children.

"First rule of laser tag ... I make the rules!" the manager declared. "You will obey my command like it is the word from on high because today, little dudes and dudettes of all stripes, I am your *laser god.*"

Taylor started giggling under his breath at the laser tag manager's theatrics, while Agatha shook her head and rolled her eyes.

"Next rule! You take them walking sticks you call legs, and you slooow them down. This combat is of the 'walking only' variety. I don't wanna be seeing no running, no crawling, and mama help you if I catch you *climbing!*" the neon-orange-haired man continued.

"Oh man, I'm gonna run and crawl *so much*," Taylor whispered excitedly to his friends.

"Running's all yours, seashell. But I'm into the crawling and I don't hear any rule against curling up on the floor and taking a nap. What about climbing?" Agatha responded to him.

"I mean, if I understood him correctly, I think we get to meet his mom if we climb on stuff. So double yes on climbing. I wanna see if her beard glows too!" Taylor answered. If the indoor-sunglasses-wearing manager overheard Elle's friends, he did a good job of ignoring them.

"And another thing! I don't got room in my cave for no dishonorable heels. I catch you covering your vest sensors? You're gone! You start shoving and punching other players? You're gone! If you pick up a smaller child and wave them around like a human shield? What happens?" the manager asked the room, waiting for a response. When he didn't get one, he crossed his arms and growled at the assembled teams. "Ain't none of you getting in there until you answer. So who wants to tell me what happens?!"

"We're gone," the players of all four teams responded in bored, uninterested unison. Elle wondered how many times a day the laser tag manager recited this exact same speech.

"That's right! You get gone! Now, remember to always . . ." The large man continued droning on, but Elle's capacity for paying attention had run empty. Distracted and bored, they looked around at the people they'd soon be competing against. The red team sat completely still. They held their laser rifles and looked straight ahead, not even glancing in the arcade worker's direction. They looked like they were about to head out to do real battle. Elle did a mental eye roll; the red team was taking the game so seriously that it went all the way back around to being even more ridiculous.

The green team was more like Elle and their friends. Some were half paying attention while others were whispering among one another. Elle didn't mean to stare, but they suddenly found it difficult to look away from one member of the green team in particular. The first thing Elle noticed about the girl was the short, electric-blue hair peeking out from under her beanie hat. She wore ripped jeans with holes around the knees and a white tank top beneath her blinking green laser tag vest that glowed in the black light. She looked bored and was staring off into space. Elle wondered what she was thinking about.

The girl suddenly and unexpectedly shifted her gaze to meet Elle's eyes. Elle was immediately flustered to the extreme. They hadn't meant to get her attention. Now she was looking at them looking at her looking at them. Elle quickly darted their eyes away as fast as they could. The interaction lasted a split second, but they were confident the embarrassment would last the rest of their life. It's not that Elle hadn't had little crushes before; they just tried their best to not do anything about them. First, they had been so busy the last year figuring themself out that they hadn't had time to have a real crush on anyone, and then afterward it all felt too complicated. Thinking about who they were interested in and who would be interested in them, it was beyond overwhelming. And every label for attraction seemed to assume that your gender was a fixed point, which for Elle it most certainly was not. Eventually, they'd decided they wanted to give up on crushes and dates and grow up to be a fantastically dressed monk, but that was easier said than done.

Elle tried to focus on anything else so they wouldn't be tempted to glance back at the girl on the green team. Agatha and Taylor were already trying to shoot each other despite the game not having started and being on the same team. The manager was explaining the importance of not staring directly into the strobe lights. And the overly serious red team were . . . still sitting completely motionless. Elle even tried counting the glowing purple light bulbs that bathed the room in the black light to try to take their mind off the girl on green team. Boredom set in fast, though, and they gave up about two-thirds of the way through their count.

Trying their best to be subtle about it, Elle snuck another glance in green team's direction. The girl looked as bored as Elle was, sitting with her elbow on her knee and chin resting on the palm of her hand. This time, Elle noticed a pin attached to the girl's beanie. It was in the shape of a heart with stripes, and while it was hard to be sure about colors under the black light, it looked like the pink, purple, and blue bands of the bisexual flag.

Elle looked down and smiled softly to themself. They knew it was a silly little crush on a stranger that wouldn't mean anything, but at least it was a crush on someone who'd accept whatever gender they were. Elle glanced back up, and was stunned to see the girl now staring back at them. This time, Elle didn't look away. They were too surprised to move, not even their eyes. A thousand thoughts overwhelmed Elle's mind. Why was she looking at them? What was she thinking? Did their eye shadow still look good? Elle could suddenly feel their own heart pounding in their chest, and each heartbeat felt like it took a hundred years.

Elle's brain computer was already malfunctioning, but it went into pure meltdown mode when the girl locked eyes across the room with them and smiled. Instantly it was a ten-car pileup crash of thoughts inside Elle's mind. Was she really smiling at them? What did it mean? They should smile back, right? Why couldn't they remember how to smile?!

Elle panicked, having no idea what to do with their face. They were certain, though, that they were blushing hard enough for their cheeks to be glowing as bright red as their nail polish. Unable to meet her gaze any longer, Elle's head turned straight down to the floor. It had just been eye contact and a smile that lasted a couple of seconds, but Elle had already replayed it in their mind a hundred times at hyperspeed. They closed their eyes and felt an uncontrollable grin take over their face. Oh, of course *now* they remembered how to smile, Elle thought to themself wryly. Elle tried to clamp down on their grinning; they'd need to defeat her just like everyone else in order to meet Nuri.

The laser tag manager must have just then finished reciting the rules that Elle wasn't paying attention to, because the spaceship doors behind him opened up. Even still sitting in the hallway, Elle could hear the pounding electronic music and see the flashing lights from within.

"So if you think you got what it takes to meet the Phantom Thief, then face the trials of the arena! Prove you're a laser *warrior* by crushing your enemies! Prove you're a laser *gentleman* by following the rules!" the man bellowed while the teams got up from the benches. Having to be very professional and very serious, red team stood up in perfect unison and marched through the doors like they were soldiers on patrol. As soon as Elle and their friends casually walked into the battleground, they were stunned with amazement. Elle felt like they had been transported to an alien world.

The room was a giant multistory maze of walls, hiding places, and smoke machines. The whole area had been painted and decorated to look like some sort of alien jungle temple. Fake foliage had been painted on the walls, and vines were wrapped around the upper-level bridges. Violet-colored runes glowed faintly on some of the maze walls. Strange, alien-looking skulls loomed over them on the walls, eyes glowing a foreboding red. Elle walked past a plastic replica of a damaged battle mecha as they took in every otherworldly detail.

"Wow . . ." they whispered softly. Elle jotted down as many mental notes about the space as they could. They were certain this would be a great setting for a new *Phantom Thief* fanfiction. As the doors started to close behind the players, the manager called out one last time, "And remember, no food or drink during the game. You wanna fill your cowardly little bellies, you better do it with *lasers!*"

"Aww, I was gonna have mid-game pizza . . ." Taylor groaned in disappointment. He reached deep into his shorts pocket and pulled out a full slice of pepperoni pizza. Elle stared at their friend in amazement. Where had he even found pizza, and how did Taylor fit so much food in his pockets? In a single bite, half the pizza slice disappeared. Taylor noticed Elle's surprise, and a sheepish expression came over him

"Wanna bite?" he asked through a mouthful of pizza, a long string of melted cheese running from his mouth to the remains of the slice.

"I'm good," Elle tersely replied. They began looking around for the direction of their blue-team base, and noticed that the members of red team had already vanished into the shadows of the maze. The players on green team seemed to have found the way to their base and they were slowly leaving the starting area. Elle watched them go, catching one last glance at the blue-haired girl. Right before she turned the corner, she looked back in Elle's direction. The girl flashed a confident smirk before raising her laser gun up at Elle and pretending to fire. Without even thinking about it, Elle put their hand to their heart like they'd really been hit. They looked down at their hand for just a moment, and when Elle looked back up, the girl had disappeared into the maze. Elle stood there watching the darkness, lost in the moment.

"...Okay. Mind telling us what *that* was about?" Agatha demanded, jolting Elle back to alertness. Elle blushed a deep scarlet; they were too frazzled to look Agatha in the eye.

"Was nothing—I don't know—shut up!" they excitedly said, tripping over their own words.

"Do you know that girl, Elle-dorado?" Taylor asked while playfully elbowing Elle in the side.

"What? No! I mean, just now before—with the rules, she was—" Elle stammered, flustered by their friends' questioning.

"Let's just find our base and come up with a strategy," they said, desperate to change the subject. Agatha and Taylor traded know-ing smirks at each other, but didn't press Elle any further about the girl on the green team.

"I'll guard the base. Someone's gotta defend it, and I don't feel like moving," Agatha offered. Elle nodded in agreement.

"Okay, sounds good. Me and Taylor will stick together and sweep the area," Elle replied, trying to use the lingo they'd picked up from the various soldier characters that had appeared in *Phantom Thief* episodes.

"We can watch each other's six so nobody can sneak up on us and . . . Where is Taylor?" they asked. The boy had managed to vanish without a trace into the smoke and shadows. Elle turned to Agatha, hoping for answers, but she just shrugged.

"Or I guess we each wander off alone by ourselves. Sure. That works too, I guess," Elle said sarcastically. They broke out into a jog down the maze while Agatha headed toward their base. They would have to win this by themself, Elle thought. But that was okay. In the end, they would reach Nuri the same way they had always figured out their nonbinary identity: on their own.

SEVENTEEN

Within moments, the game had begun and Elle had been forced to dodge, duck, dip, dive, and doge through a maelstrom of laser fire. The air was full of green, red, blue and yellow lasers, the beams made visible by the thick mist that filled the room.

Elle rounded a corner of the maze, but then quickly ducked back when they saw a boy wearing a green vest sprinting down the corridor. He was being chased by one of the older teens on red team. Or at least, Elle thought he was. They could see the red laser fire, but no bright red lights on a vest. The mystery revealed itself once the two ran past Elle. They could see that the much taller teenager had covered up the lights on his vest with black tape. Without those lights, he was nearly invisible from more than a few feet away. A wave of anger surged within Elle.

The line between charming trickery and outright cheating was a fine one, but Elle was quite certain these teens had crossed it. What happened to honor among Phantom Thieves? What happened to the sanctity of *laser tag*? This was a new kind of low. Elle decided that on the off chance they couldn't win, they'd at least make sure that the red team lost.

Elle sprang out from the corner right behind the black-clad teen. From this close, they could still make out where the targets on the vest were supposed to be. They squeezed the plastic trigger; their blue laser had no problem getting through the teenager's cheater tape. Elle couldn't see the blinking lights that would normally signify that they'd scored a hit, but they did hear the buzzing sound effect. If they needed any further confirmation that their shot had found its mark, they got it when the almost-an-adult suddenly stopped, turned around to face them, and angrily punched the nearby maze wall. Elle stuck their tongue out at the sore loser and gleefully ran off. The joy of victory put an extra bounce in their step as they continued on.

From there, Elle did their best to score points and disrupt the other teams. They'd managed to sneakily score some hits by firing from behind an alien statue, but lasers from the second story above had forced them back into the maze for cover. Elle was powered by adrenaline and exhilaration. No game of laser tag had ever had such high stakes before. Knowing that every beam of light could be the difference between meeting Nuri Grena or not was both terrifying and exciting.

Hiding among the foliage on the second floor, Elle could see the members of yellow team below cut down by the invisible shadows that should have been glowing red. Elle gritted their teeth in frustration. If nobody stopped them soon, the red team would run away with this match, and the statuette. But if Elle could find the red team's base, then maybe they could score some serious points against them.

Moments later, Elle was down on the ground floor and stepping onto a fake boulder. From there, they could gaze over the top of the maze wall to find the path to red team's base. But while they were searching, they were suddenly startled by a voice to their right.

"Hitbylaserssayswhat?!" shouted a sharp, lively voice. Elle turned to see who was calling out to them, and barely got out a "huh?"

before losing their balance on the boulder. They tripped over their own feet, and tumbled back down onto the ground. Before they could get up, the girl from the green team was standing over them.

"Hi, my name's Dawn," she said, and fired a laser blast right at Elle's heart.

Beedle-lee-bee! Their vest jingled as the blue lights blinked on and off to show that they'd been hit. Elle wasn't sure whether to groan from the pain of falling or smile at the sight of Dawn.

"Sorry 'bout making you fall. Just meant to surprise you, not hurt you. Are you okay?" she said, offering Elle a hand. Elle gratefully took it, and she helped pull them back up onto their feet. Something about her having shot Elle before making sure they were okay made them like her even more.

"Yeah, I'm fine. No worries. I'm Elle, by the way," they replied bashfully. Elle wondered if Dawn would run off now that she had scored a hit on them, but she didn't. She was staying where she was.

"So, umm—uhh, how's the game going?" Elle asked, unsure what to say.

Dawn shrugged and smiled. "Not too bad. I saw this one kid fall off a rock. That was pretty funny. Figured I'd stick around, see if they do better when they're actually on their feet," she answered.

Her effortless use of they and their pronouns sent Elle's heart aflutter. They didn't know what to say; they could only smile. Dawn met their gaze, and held it for what felt like forever until the lights on Elle's vest lit up and once again glowed a bright blue. Dawn cocked an eyebrow and raised her blaster. The battle was on.

Elle rolled out of the way of the green laser and fired back at Dawn. To Elle's surprise, she darted out of the way and kicked off the fake boulder into the air. Elle fired a few blue lasers, but couldn't hit the girl leaping toward them. Dawn landed low, knees bent. Then, like a coiled spring, she kicked off and rushed toward Elle. She darted in close, too close for Elle to get a shot on her with their laser blaster. Dawn jammed her own blaster right into Elle's vest—she was trying to hit them from point-blank range. With their free hand, Elle just barely managed to swat her laser rifle away. Dawn's laser went wide, missing the sensors on Elle's vest by mere inches. Elle was surprised by how vigorously Dawn was fighting against them, but it was nothing short of thrilling. Joy and adrenaline overtook them; they couldn't remember the last time they'd had so much fun.

While Elle still had a hand on Dawn's blaster, she managed to grab their own laser rifle. The two grappled, neither willing to let the other get a shot in. Elle and Dawn paused only briefly to lock eyes and smile at each other before their competitive grimaces returned. The pair spun around, and the surprise of her back hitting a maze wall made Dawn let go of Elle's blaster. Sensing an opportunity for victory, Elle leapt back a few feet to create distance between them. They raised their blaster and smirked; this round would go to them.

Or at least, that's what Elle had thought. Suddenly and without warning, Dawn dropped down to the ground. Before Elle could even realize what was happening, she shot out her leg, and Elle felt it hook around the back of their foot. Dawn quickly pulled her leg back, and sent Elle tumbling to the ground. It all happened so fast, Elle was stunned by surprise as much as they were by the fall. And once more, for the second time in as many minutes, Dawn was standing over Elle with a laser rifle pointed at their chest.

"Sorry, that time I *did* mean to knock you down," she confidently said with a wink.

Elle looked up at Dawn, flustered in more ways than one. "Where . . . where did you learn *that?*" they asked. Was it dance? Martial arts? Whatever it was, Dawn being able to do it made her even cooler in Elle's eyes.

"Capoeira. You should try it," she cheerfully replied. Capo-what? Elle had no idea what she was referring to, but yeah, they definitely wanted to try it.

"Well, this has been fun, but . . ." Dawn said, brushing a strand of bright blue hair from out of her face. She started to squeeze the trigger on her blaster when suddenly a trio of near-invisible, all-black-wearing teenagers emerged from the shadows and opened fire on them both.

"Darn it!" Dawn exclaimed through gritted teeth as she leapt around a maze corner to dodge the incoming laser beams. A disoriented Elle scrambled to their feet and stumbled to the opposite corner a few feet away from Dawn. While they ran, Elle saw red laser dots dance across their arm. It was a miracle they got to cover without their vest sensors being hit.

"Ugh! These guys! I mean, what kind of jerks cheat at *laser tag?*" Elle called out to Dawn. The two were separated by a few feet of maze, and the endless barrage of lasers that filled the space between them.

"Blegh, tell me about it. One of them is my stupid older brother," Dawn replied with an aggravated roll of her eyes. "I'm gonna be *so mad* if him and his jerk-face friends win again," she said.

"We'll just have to beat them, then," Elle answered with a smile. They popped their head out from the wall they were hiding behind, and fired a few blasts at the red team attackers. For the next few minutes, Elle and Dawn traded volleys with the older teens. It was a stalemate; the red team couldn't get close enough to hit the two thirteen-year-olds, and the pair couldn't risk leaving their cover. Even when they could fire their blasters, it was almost impossible to aim with the red team's sensor lights covered up. Elle looked at their temporary ally; something about the sight of Dawn firing a laser gun and shouting obscenities at her brother made Elle's heart skip a beat.

"I, umm . . . I like your hair," Elle stammered, so nervous they thought they'd blush so hard that their head would explode. "It's a . . . it's a really cool color," they hastily added.

Dawn stopped firing her blaster and turned to look at Elle. She looked surprised, but then smiled widely. "Thanks! My dad helped me dye it," she said, looking down at the ground and curling a strand of blue hair around her finger.

"Umm . . . I think, I mean—I really like your dress." For the first time in the brief span that Elle had known her, Dawn sounded nervous herself. Elle looked down at their dress, thankful that the green lights on their vest brought out the jade color of their dress.

"It's my favorite one! Not something I can always wear to school, but I wanted to wear it for the Nuri Grena signing today," they explained. Elle tried to sound casual, but inside they were beaming that Dawn had complimented their dress.

"So you're big into *Phantom Thief*?" Dawn asked while firing her blaster down the corridor.

"Yeah! I mean—it's my favorite show, but you know. It's cool. How about you?" Elle tried their best to play it cool. They worried it might be off-putting if they fell into mega fan-enby mode.

"I've seen a few seasons. It's fun! But to be honest, after I win I'm gonna sell the collectible so I can buy a new skateboard," Dawn answered breezily.

"I'm . . . probably gonna have to find room for it since my shelves are already full of *Phantom Thief* stuff."

"Oh, so you're *that* kind of fan," Dawn said with a playful smile.

"Well . . . okay, yeah, you got me. But it's not just the show. It's *them*. The actor, Nuri Grena," Elle said. They were growing more bashful the more they talked, but the words were pouring out too fast now and Elle couldn't stop themself.

"They . . . they had a really big impact on me. Helped me figure a lot of stuff out. Heck, I'm supposed to be at detention right now, but I snuck out just to meet them," they continued.

"Seriously? That's awesome!"

"I mean—it's just . . . they just seem so confident. Like they got it all together. If I could talk to them, I think . . . I'm sorry, I'm rambling. It's just kinda—"

"They helped you realize you're nonbinary?" Dawn said, finishing Elle's thought for them. "I'm sorry—I shouldn't assume. I didn't ask your pronouns. If I got it wrong I'm—" she nervously stammered out, but now it was Elle's turn to helpfully interrupt.

"No, don't be sorry! You're right. I am nonbinary. I use they and them. And . . . yeah. It was Nuri Grena who helped me put it all together. Seeing them as Phantom Thief, this super-cool hero who was both genders and neither gender and . . . it just . . . it *made sense* to me, ya know?"

"Oh, I totally know. For me it was when I was watching that old cartoon about the element people with the cool martial arts. I was like, oh dang . . . fire boy's cute. And then I was like, oh dang . . . water girl's cute too. And then it was just this *relief* when the metal girl had a crush on them both. It let me know that being bi really was a thing, and that it was okay for me to be bi. So yeah, I get it," Dawn replied.

Elle was surprised in the most pleasant of ways. They had told so many people about how *Phantom Thief* helped them find their identity, and most people either thought they were joking or nodded along without really understanding. But here was someone who not only got where Elle was coming from, she had her own tale to tell about finding herself within stories. The two tweens stared into each other's eyes, and for a moment, the maze and electro music and laser blasts all disappeared. There was nothing in the whole world other than the two of them.

"They stopped firing! Charge 'em!" one of the boys from red

team shouted. Their perfect moment rudely interrupted, Elle looked down the hall to see the three members of red team sprinting toward them.

"Dang it!" Dawn shouted. Longing gazes would have to come later, for now the two had to focus on fending off their approaching opponents. For people who had been total strangers mere minutes ago, Elle and Dawn were an effective team. They couldn't score any hits on the red team, but at least they forced the older players to stop and hide behind cover. Elle kept firing their blaster down the hall, but their thoughts soon turned back to Dawn. The way she had knocked him down when they had been sparring, Elle couldn't get it out of their head.

"Hey, when you dropped on the floor and tripped me, what'd you say that was again? Capybara?" Elle asked over the *pew pew* sounds of the laser blasters. Dawn shook her head and laughed. Elle wasn't sure what was funny, but they liked making Dawn laugh.

"Heh, those are the big rats who're best friends with all the other animals. It's capoeira. Cap-o-era," she responded, slowly pronouncing the syllable. "It's like this half dance, half martial arts style from Brazil. Lots of cartwheels and jump kicks and stuff. It's super fun! I just learned that leg sweep I did on you last week. It's called a *corta capim*. You should for real try out a class, I train after school on Tuesdays and Thursdays," she cheerfully invited them.

Elle let the idea roll around in their head. It had only been a few short hours ago that they were in the batting cage, frustrated about not being able to play more sports. Maybe this was the solution. It sounded fun from the way Dawn described it, and getting to see her more would certainly be a bonus, but old worries still echoed heavily in Elle's mind.

"I . . . it sounds cool, but . . . would it be okay for me to do it? With being nonbinary, I mean. Feels like since I came out, I'm the wrong 'me' for whatever team I try," Elle said softly, unable to hide the tired sadness in their voice.

"You don't have to worry about that at all, trust me. Only thing you need to do to belong is be there. Promise," Dawn replied reassuringly. "Doesn't matter your age, or your gender, or nothing like that. Everybody trains together and fights together. We don't even divide by experience. Very first time I tried capoeira, I had to fight the club champion! He cartwheel kicked me right across the face.

It. Was. *Awesome!*" she said with a wild glee. The more Elle heard about capoeira, the more exciting it sounded. Maybe this really was a sport where Elle wouldn't have to worry about their identity not matching their teammates'; they could simply be themself and run and jump until they were exhausted. Elle felt a rush of relief and excitement just thinking about it.

"Maybe I will give it a try. I mean, how could I say no to kicks to the face?" Elle said with a grin.

"You should! It's a heck of a lot more fun than staying still during laser tag and WAITING FOR YOUR BROTHER'S ANNOYING LOSER FRIENDS TO LEAVE YOU THE FRICK ALONE!" she angrily shouted at the players on red team, who had not stopped firing at Elle and Dawn the entire time the pair had been talking. Slowly but surely, they had marched farther and farther down the hall, and soon there would be no place for Elle and Dawn to hide.

"I think they got us pinned down," Elle said bitterly. They could barely poke their head out from behind the maze wall without having to shield their eyes from red laser lights.

"Yeah, looks that way . . Wanna go out in a blaze of glory, though?" Dawn asked with a grin. She raised up her laser blaster, ready to go down fighting. Elle nodded, making a heroic last stand against the shadowy forces of evil had *"Phantom Thief* episode" written all over it.

The two leapt out into the hallway, screaming their tiny battle cries and wildly firing lasers down the hall. For a few seconds, it was a dizzying blur of blue, green, and red beams firing in every which way. Suddenly, though, Elle heard a panicked yell that cut through the noise and chaos of the battle.

"Aaaagghhhh!"—*WHUMP!*

The scream came to a sudden stop when a person fell hard into the ground behind the red team players. Elle looked up to try to find where the person fell from, perhaps the bridge or upper levels of the arena space. The fallen figure unsteadily got back onto his feet. Elle was shocked when he got up, and revealed a vest full of blinking blue lights.

"Taylor?!" they exclaimed in surprise. Elle was bewildered to see their friend suddenly standing before them. The equally taken aback teenagers on red team were now surrounded, and unsure which direction to focus their fire on.

"Get 'em," Dawn loudly yelled, letting loose on the hapless teens.

Elle and Taylor joined her, and now they were the ones on the offensive. The familiar *beedle-lee-bee* sounds jingled through the air as Elle, Dawn, and Taylor scored hit after hit on the red team players until they ran off back toward their base. Elle stopped firing once they had fled, and traded a triumphant high five with Dawn. They weren't sure if their hands really did touch for a split second longer than was normal for a high five, or if it was just in Elle's imagination. Next, they rushed forward and gave Taylor a big, squeezy hug.

"Taylor, that was amazing! You totally took them by surprise. Where did you even fall from?" Elle excitedly asked their friend.

"I don't know!" he replied with an energetic shrug. Elle had more questions for him, but they suddenly didn't matter when they heard that *beedle-lee-bee* sound again and both their vests started blinking on and off. They turned around to face Dawn, who was pointing her blaster at them with a mischievous smile across her face. Elle's mouth hung open, but no noise came out. Their team-up was already over.

"Don't take those pretty eyes off an opponent," she advised them. "And don't worry. I'll just take the statue, and you can meet the actor after *I* win the game," Dawn teased before running off deeper into the maze.

Elle stood bolted to the ground. They didn't even try to chase after her.

"What are you smiling about?" Taylor asked, noting the happy look on Elle's face. Elle turned to him, glad the room was too dark for Taylor to see how deep they were blushing,

"She said my eyes were pretty."

EIGHTEEN

After the match had ended, Elle and their friends had rushed to the leaderboard to see the results. Elle anxiously jumped up and down, trying to see the screen over the taller players. As the results popped onto the screen one by one, Elle felt the frustrating sting of defeat when their blue team finished in third. But they soon felt no small amount of satisfaction when the red team came next, only having managed to come in second. Dawn's green team had taken the top spot, and as the team's highest scorer she would take home the prize. Elle's heart skipped a beat—partially out of gooey-crush-admiration of Dawn, and mostly because her winning meant that Elle would finally get to meet Nuri!

Dawn walked away with a valuable collectible, and Elle walked away with her social media info and a promise to join her at the next capoeira class. While part of Elle wanted to spend the rest of the day with Dawn, their excitement to meet Nuri felt like jolts of electricity all through their body.

Elle, Agatha, and Taylor rushed to the front of the arcade, special pass in hand. The big digital clock on the wall was a constant reminder of how little time Elle had left before detention was over. But when they reached the brightly lit prize counter, there was nobody there but Agatha's nemesis, Roger.

"Hey, Roger! Where's the big star? Make with the celebrity, pimple breath," Agatha barked at the exasperated arcade worker.

"Too late, ya little gremlin!" he shouted back with relish.

"Um—no. We have the pass to meet them." Elle held up the slip of paper.

Roger leaned over the glass counter and plucked it from their hand. "They dashed out a couple minutes ago. You took too long with the lasers, and they had to go to their next signing," he smugly sneered at Agatha.

Elle balled up their fists. "But they're *supposed* to be here."

"And *I'm* supposed to have a million bucks and be dating an influencer. Life isn't fair, kid." Elle's face flushed hot with anger. After everything the day had thrown at them, Elle wanted to scream. They felt like a rubber band that was perilously close to snapping.

"Okay, well then, give us Petunia to make up for it. Fair's fair!" Agatha cried.

"Not on your life, little girl. Here, if you get out and don't come back during my next five shifts, I'll give you a glow-in-the-dark eyeball," the arcade worker offered with an aggravated eye roll. Agatha glared right at him, but reached over and took the rubber eyeball without another word.

"So . . . back to the bookstore?" Taylor asked, already bouncing Agatha's new eyeball prize off the arcade floor. By the time he finished speaking, Elle had already blown past him, powered by determination and rage.

"Bookstore!"

✿✿✿

After a few minutes of furious scootering back to the Purple Prose, Elle had calmed down enough to bring up a question that had been gnawing at them since the laser tag.

"Hey, Taylor, I gotta ask. I still don't get where you went during the match. How'd you just disappear like that at the start of the game?" Elle asked once they'd reached the bookstore's parking lot. Taylor's face lit up with an excited energy as he began his explanation.

"It was crazy! You gotta hear about it. Turns out I was some sorta *chosen one* and I got dragged through a portal to the Lazer Kingdom!" Taylor said. Elle stopped dead in their tracks, unable to both walk and process Taylor's strange comment at the same time.

"I'm sorry. You did . . . what?" Elle asked disbelievingly.

"I rescued the Photon Princess from the Neon Dragon and stopped the evil skateboard wizard Radocles!"

"Okay. Sure you did," Agatha said, her voice heavy with sarcasm.

"If you don't want to tell us, that's fine. You don't have to make something up," Elle added.

Taylor balled up his fists and stomped on the parking lot concrete. "For real, you guys. *I saved the world!*" Elle and Agatha traded eye rolls, head shakes, and sighs, then continued on past him into the bookshop. By now the signing was well underway, and the line that had been outside earlier had disappeared.

Elle quickly shuffled through the doors, and was welcomed with the comforting familiarity of their favorite spot in town. The sound of turning pages, the smell of coffee from the café, row after row of so many books it felt like it went on forever—it all put Elle so completely at ease.

That ease was shattered by a piercing voice that Elle would have known even in the deepest of nightmares.

"Well, where are they, then?!" cried the unmistakable sound of one Susan Campbell. Hearing their mother's voice, Elle's blood turned to ice in their veins. Elle looked around the bookstore in a panic, desperately trying to find where their mother could be. The way her voice could bounce off walls like a spring, she could be anywhere. Why was she here? Did she know that Elle was skipping detention? They quickly looked over their shoulder, half expecting to find an enraged Susan Campbell sanding right behind them and ready to strike.

"Was that—?" Taylor whispered, sharing Elle's dread. Elle nodded, too afraid to make a sound. They wanted to hide, but they didn't know where. They felt a tug on the sleeve of their dress, and looked to see Agatha gesturing for them to follow her.

Soon, the three were squished behind a big, comfy, velvety chair in the bookstore's reading area. Agatha pointed toward the nearby in-store café, where Susan looked impatient to order while beside her, Jerome hungrily scanned the café's section of brightly colored cupcakes and pastries.

"I saw your mom and her dude-guy-friend going into the café when we came in," Agatha explained.

"I heard her ask 'where are they.' She has to be here looking for me," Elle muttered with crushing despair. "She's gonna drag me back to school and ground me until high school."

"Shh!" Agatha put her finger to her lips and hushed Elle. "Hold on a second."

"I'm serious! Where are they?" they heard Susan repeat. But then Elle's mother pointed up to the large painting on the wall behind the café counter.

"If you're gonna paint a mural showing famous authors drinking coffee together, but you leave out Toni Morrison and Margaret Atwood, then what's even the point?!" Susan bellowed. Jerome said something to her that Elle couldn't overhear, but it prompted their mother to shout, "It's the principle!"

"So she's . . . not here looking for you?" Taylor said with a note of confusion. Elle shook their head but hesitated to say anything. They simply watched, and tried to understand. Susan and Jerome seemed too busy looking into each other's eyes to be looking for Elle. Elle could just barely see them holding hands while they waited in line. They had never seen their mother and her boyfriend out by themselves. The couple looked . . . happy. Really happy. Elle felt a pang of guilt. They'd shut out Jerome because they had assumed he'd leave eventually, but that . . . that didn't seem like the look of a guy who planned on taking off. Maybe they owed it to their mother to give him a real chance.

But then, if they weren't here to hunt Elle down, then what were they doing at the Purple Prose?

"Oh no," they whispered to themself as realization set in.

"I think . . . I think they're here for the *same reason* we are," Elle said, slinking back behind the large chair. They took in a deep breath. "I think they're here for the *Nuri Grena signing*," they whispered, their heart coldly gripped by fear.

"Aww! She must be getting you a book signed since you're . . . ya know. 'In detention,'" Taylor said, throwing finger quotes around the last few words. "That's so sweet of her!" He beamed.

Elle let out a sigh and tried to mentally work through this latest development. A swirling mix of appreciation and dread churned within them.

"It *is* sweet, but it's a whole 'nother thing to worry about! Now I gotta be sneaking around even in the bookstore," Elle complained. "Do you guys think you could distract my mom long enough for me to meet Nuri?" they asked their friends. It wasn't much of a plan, but if there was anyone Elle could trust to pull it off, it was Taylor and Agatha.

"Oh, we got this, little flower," Agatha replied confidently. "Ready to be the most annoying kid you can be, seashell?" she asked Taylor.

"Literally born for it," he said in response. Elle watched Taylor and Agatha roll out from behind the chair and scamper off to the bookstore café. Taylor bounded up the short set of stairs to the coffee counter, then stopped in fake surprise.

"Ms. Campbell?! What are *you* doing here?" he exclaimed in an over-the-top manner. Susan Campbell looked at him with a blank, confused expression.

"Huh? Taylor? Umm—I'm here getting a book signed for Elle. Are you here with your parents?" she asked. Before Susan could get a handle on what was going on, Agatha was suddenly there in front of her as well, bombarding her with words.

"Ms. Campbell, the bookstore lady said I'm too young to buy nine different true crime novels. Can you come tell her it's okay and that it's research? Don't ask what it's research for, though," she quickly said in a single breath.

"Agatha?" Susan muttered in confusion. "You're here too? What are—"

"Ms. Campbell, are you gonna get a pastry? What kind are you gonna get?" Taylor interrupted.

"Ms. Campbell, how many different kinds of pastry flavors are there? Do they all have jelly inside?" he added, keeping up the barrage of questions.

"Ms. Campbell, can you name all the different jelly flavors? There's grape, and strawberry, and raspberry, and marmly-made, and . . ."

Elle didn't stick around to hear the rest of the list. They quickly scurried off toward the bookshop's science-fiction section, satisfied that their friends were more than up to the task of keeping their mother distracted.

On a normal trip to the bookshop, Elle could spend an entire hour just going up and down the rows of novels, comics, and guidebooks. Whole afternoons had been lost admiring the art on countless book covers and reading the story summaries on the back. But this wasn't a normal Saturday stroll through the racks of books. Time was of the essence, and Elle had a mission to accomplish. They needed to grab a book for Nuri to sign, then find the star of the show. They ignored the rows of romance novels and the buff, long-haired men, each more shirtless than the last, that graced their covers, and didn't give so much as a glance to the table full of art books that promised to teach them how to paint like Vincent van Gogh. Instead, Elle made a beeline to where they knew the *Phantom Thief* books would be.

While *Phantom Thief* may have started as a television show, over the decades the long-running series had branched off into countless spin-offs and side stories in other mediums. There were books, comics, audio dramas, and one disastrous Broadway musical that the fan base had agreed to never speak of again.

Elle slowed down their speed walking as they reached their destination, an entire shelf of books dedicated to their favorite time-traveling heist adventure franchise. This part of the store was deserted, save for a boy a few inches taller than Elle whose head was hidden in a book. Elle started scanning the titles on the shelf, trying to find the perfect one for Nuri to sign. Their first instinct was to grab a novel starring Grena's Ninth Thief character. But the actor hadn't written it; it was just about a character they played. No, better to find the graphic novel that Nuri had written themself, Elle decided.

After a few moments of searching, Elle found a title they hadn't seen before, and excitedly pulled it off the shelf. A surge of excitement coursed through them when they saw "NURI GRENA" on the cover in big, bold letters. This was it, the comic that had brought Elle's hero to their hometown.

They examined the cover. It was Nuri's Ninth Thief teaming up with the Disco Robot from the very first Phantom Thief's Corporeal Crew back in the 70s. Elle's eyes widened with excitement; their little superfan mind started racing with theories about the story within. Elle hungrily opened the book, and made it three pages in before they had to mentally force themself to focus. For once in their life, escaping into fiction wasn't the answer. The answers they needed were right there in the real world.

With renewed purpose, Elle tucked the graphic novel under their arm and proudly stepped toward the signing area ... where they immediately walked straight into the boy reading a book. The boy dropped his book in surprise, and Elle tumbled back onto the ground.

"Sorry about that! I wasn't looking where I was going. Here, let me get your book. Seriously, *so* sorry for ..." an embarrassed Elle said, hurrying to pick themself up and return the fallen book. But when they looked up to give it back, Elle's jaw dropped with utter shock. They hadn't walked into a boy at all; it was ...

"... CASEY?!" Elle exclaimed. Sure enough, standing before them was Casey Strick, the Mean Queen of Broderick Middle School. But it wasn't Casey like Elle had ever seen her before. Gone were her stylish blouses, sweaters, and skirts, replaced instead by cargo shorts and a baggy, ill-fitting rugby shirt. Her long blond hair was carefully hidden under a baseball hat. She looked nothing at all like the girl who so often tormented Elle for their loud fashion and nerdy interests. Looking down at Elle, Casey's face rapidly cycled through a flurry of emotions. First came surprise, then for a millisecond she was awash with fear, before finally settling on anger.

"You! What are you doing here?" she said in an accusatory tone.

"Me? What are *you* doing here?!" Elle responded with indignation as they scrambled back onto their feet.

"You're supposed to be in detention! Becky Garcia filmed Mr. McMullins getting you in trouble! She added a trombone sound effect when you got really sad. It was *hilarious.*"

"I . . . kinda snuck out," Elle reluctantly admitted, unable to come up with even a halfway believable lie. "But hey! I thought you said *Phantom Thief* is for dorks."

"It is! But . . . well, it's still cool to have a real *TV star* come to your town. And I checked out the show a little, and . . . I really like fancy suits the actor wears, okay?" Casey could only mutter the last part under her breath, and was unable to look Elle in the eye. Elle had never seen Casey look so vulnerable before. It was strange to see.

"You're still a nerd for being so obsessed with it, though," she hastily added. Ah, there was the Casey Strick that Elle knew and begrudgingly endured.

"You know, it's weirder that you're *not* a nerd. Everyone's a nerd," Elle shot back at her. Casey didn't throw back a retort. For once, the razor-tongued popular girl was speechless. Her eyes were darting around, clearly afraid that someone else would notice her. Elle wasn't used to seeing Casey not completely in control of her surroundings. Elle looked closer at her outfit. It was undeniably masculine, almost clumsily so. Like someone's uncertain idea of how a thirteen-year-old boy should dress. Elle recognized the fearful, on-guard look on Casey's face all too well. It was the exact same way they had looked the first times Elle had gone out in a dress or makeup.

"So . . . you like the suits they wear. And—well . . . I haven't seen you dress like this at school before . . ." Elle softly said. It was the most delicate wording they could think of to address the metaphorical elephant in the room. Casey's face turned a bright red, and her gaze turned sharply down to the ground.

"Let's just say you're not the only one who's trying to figure stuff out . . ." she whispered to Elle as softly as she could. As soon as the words left her mouth, Casey nervously stuffed her hands into the gargantuan pockets of her cargo shorts. It occurred to Elle that Casey had probably gone nearly her whole life without wearing pants with pockets. Maybe this brought her some measure of comfort and euphoria, just like Elle had felt the first time they'd gotten to spin around in a skirt. Elle smiled warmly. For the first time ever, they saw something of themself in their middle school rival. Casey scowled, clearly not used to receiving compassion from Elle.

"Ugh, don't look at me like that. You're making it worse. Look, I'll make you a deal. If you don't tell anyone that I was here or that I'm dressed like this, I won't tell anyone you ditched detention," she said with a desperate sigh. Elle put their hands on their hips and shot her a disbelieving look. Elle may not have liked Casey very much, but there were lines they would never, ever cross.

"Okay, A—I would *never* tell anyone about what you're going through. This is *your* journey. You should only tell *who* you want, *when* you want. But B—if you could still not tell anyone I ditched, that'd be super cool of you, pretty please," Elle said. Elle hoped

Casey wouldn't tattle on them, but even if she did, it would be worth it knowing they had done the right thing.

"Ugh, just get outta here before someone sees us. Nerd," Casey said. She rolled her eyes at Elle, but couldn't hide the smile that crept across her face. Elle nodded and scampered away. They weren't sure how things would be with Casey after this, but Elle felt like things had changed forever between the two of them. Who knows, maybe this was the start of an enemy becoming a frenemy.

NINETEEN

All day long, Elle had tried to prepare themself for the moment they would see their hero in person. But when they turned the corner and saw Nuri Grena mere feet away, no amount of preparation would have been enough. Elle felt the breath completely leave their body. They were really here. The Phantom Thief themself was *here!* Right in front of them! Not on a faraway television screen—in real life! Elle knew in their head that Nuri Grena wasn't really a magical time-bending super thief, but, well . . . they sure did look like the character they played, and they sure did sound like the character they played.

Sitting behind the table, flashing a radiant smile and signing books, it looked to Elle like the actor-slash-author-slash-activist was literally glowing. Their scarlet suit dazzled against their copper complexion. Nuri had on golden lipstick and their eye shadow was a brilliant mix of red, yellow, and orange. In Elle's mind, Nuri Grena was like if the sun itself had stepped down from the sky and taken a human form. Elle knew they needed to force themself to move, otherwise they would spend the rest of the day staring in open-jawed awe.

Elle squeezed the graphic novel they were holding in their hands, and quickly gave themself a light smack on the forehead with it. Just hard enough to pull them free from the sinking quicksand of their own thoughts. They forced their legs to move again, and finally took their place at the back of the line. By now, there were only a few people still waiting. In a few short minutes, there would be no one left but Elle and their hero. They could feel their heart pounding like thunder in their chest. The last time they had been this nervous was when they had asked everyone at school to use their real name.

From the back of the line, Elle stood on their tiptoes so they could get a better view of the store. They glanced over at the café, and were relieved to see that Agatha and Taylor were still keeping their mother plenty distracted. With that worry off their mind, they could focus on what they were going to say to Nuri.

What should they open with? Elle thought. They could cut to the chase and ask what the best way to stand up for themself and their gender was, but that was probably too strong to start with. What if they just said they were a big fan of the show? Ugh, too generic, they decided. Nuri Grena had spent all day talking to "big fans" of the show. Maybe Elle could start with a thank-you. It was important they got to tell Nuri how big an impact they had made on Elle. Yeah, that was it. It was perfect, Elle thought. It was personal, but meaningful, and didn't put too much pressure on Nuri for a response.

They had the book, they knew what to say—Elle had it all figured out. They were next in line now, and Grena was finishing up with the woman in front of them. Elle was really about to meet Nuri Grena. This was happening. They could do this.

And then the star of *Phantom Thief* looked up right at Elle, gave them a friendly wave, and cheerily said, "Hi there! Do you have a book you'd like me to sign? Bring it here and I'll give ya the ol' autograph-a-rooni! It's the only bit of cursive I know how to write, and I don't mean to brag, but it's *super* loopy."

Elle Campbell could not do this.

They felt like bowling balls had been tied to their feet. Their mouth felt like a whole roll of duct tape had been put over it. They had to move. Why couldn't they move?! Nuri Grena was staring *right at them*. This person who meant everything to them had always been a world away. Now they were close enough to reach out and touch, and Elle felt completely overwhelmed. Time had slowed to a crawl while also simultaneously going at super speed. The room started spinning out of control as Elle desperately tried to will themself to speak, but the knots in their stomach twisted tighter and tighter in their gut. After everything their friends had gone through to help them get here, and now they were blowing it! Elle wanted to shut their eyes and run away, when suddenly a large hand clasped them gently on the shoulder.

"Hi, Mx. Grena! It is Mx., right? Like 'mix?' I wanna make sure I get it right." Elle looked up to see none other than Jerome smiling and standing over them. Terror ran down Elle's spine like lightning. Their mother's boyfriend had caught them red-handed. First they'd frozen in front of their hero, and now they were likely to be grounded for the rest of middle school. But then to Elle's surprise, Jerome looked down at them and gave a reassuring wink.

"Yup, you got it right! Appreciate you asking. Nice to meet you . . ." Nuri Grena replied with a charming smile.

"Oh, I'm Jerome. But right now I'm just the hype man for this little champion of awesome right here," he answered excitedly. He gently shook Elle the tiniest bit by the shoulders, and Elle felt the knot in their stomach start to relax.

"Now you've probably been talking all day to people saying they're your biggest fan, but trust me. All of them are *chump change* next to this one right here. If it's *Phantom Thief,* they know it. They are the real deal superfan, ain't that right?" Jerome said, looking down at Elle.

A thin smile grew across Elle's face, battling back their nervousness and fear. They nodded their head up and down enthusiastically. They hadn't quite found their voice yet, but they were getting there. Nuri clapped their hands with excitement and motioned for Elle to come closer to the table.

"Oh well heck yeah! I'm always down to talk to a superfan. What's your name?" they asked. Elle looked up quickly at Jerome, who provided a reassuring nod. Elle stepped forward, and shook their hero's hand.

"I'm Elle," they said, trying their best to keep their voice steady and calm. This was really happening. They were really talking to Nuri Grena!

"That's a pretty name, I like it a lot," the actor replied. Their voice was as full of sunshine as their makeup.

"Thanks! I picked it myself," Elle said bashfully, but with pride. While everything in Elle screamed at them to go full fan mode, they tried their best to clamp down on that instinct.

"How has the signing been for you today, Mx. Grena?" they asked as calmly and respectfully as they could.

"Aww, you don't gotta be calling me 'Mx. Grena' like we're in school or something like that. Just call me Nuri. 'Kay, Elle?" the celebrity cheerfully replied, leaning back in their chair and running their fingers through their short, pixie-cut hair. Elle nodded, and tried not to freak out about Nuri Grena knowing their name.

"The signing has been good," Nuri said. "This one girl spent ten minutes pitching to me her idea for an episode where a corgi in an astronaut costume went to a moon populated by alien guinea pigs. She had the whole thing storyboarded out as Instagram pics!" Elle started giggling at Nuri's story, and they merrily continued, "I'd have done the episode, but I hear the guinea pigs have a real shark for an agent, and I don't think *Phantom Thief* has a big enough budget for that kind of star power."

"Maybe they're rare guinea pigs that Phantom Thief steals from the Menagerie of Madness, and then they get loose in the Getaway Hearse," Elle playfully suggested. Nuri lightly smacked the table with their hand, then excitedly pointed at Elle.

"Now *that's* a good idea! We oughta get you in the writers' room one day. So you watch the show a lot?" Nuri asked.

"I never miss an episode! And I went back and watched the old stuff. I mean, all the old episodes that are publicly available. They destroyed every physical copy of the Third Thief's two-hour Berlin Wall Spectacular from 1989," Elle excitedly answered before stopping themself. They could feel themself starting to ramble. Elle took in a deep, calming breath. This time, they really did want to gather the right words, and speak from the heart.

"Sorry. The show . . . to be honest, it means *the world* to me. I feel like I grew up in that universe. Any time real life got too overwhelming, I could escape to another adventure. I hope this isn't too much to say, but before you came on the show I was . . . I was really confused . . . a lot. Everyone else seemed so *certain* of who I was supposed to be just because of how I was born, and it all felt so wrong. I had no idea who I wanted to be. And then you became the Phantom Thief, and you were so confident, and so . . . so . . . yourself!" Elle exclaimed. They had so much more to say, but wanted to make sure they weren't freaking out Nuri. But they were still looking deep into Elle's eyes, and they kept nodding intently as Elle told their story. Elle continued:

"The episode where your Thief character talks to the order of Cyber Nuns who raised them, the flutter of joy they described every time someone referred to them as 'they,' how they felt both like a boy and a girl and like neither, how they just wanted to be themself, whatever that meant—it felt like you put into words everything I didn't know I had been feeling. Without you . . . without you I don't think I ever could have come out as nonbinary. So thank you. From the bottom of my heart times a *million*—thank you."

Elle took what felt like the deepest breath of their life. Even if Nuri didn't have any deeper answers for them, at the very least Elle had gotten to properly thank the person who had already done so much for them. They turned back to look at Jerome, who smiled and returned a reassuring thumbs-up. And then, to Elle's surprise, Nuri Grena reached out and clasped Elle's hands within their own.

"Hey, you *never* need to thank me. Do you know how brave and amazing it is to find and embrace your real self? You did that. *You.* I'm glad I could help, but that courage was in you all along," they said with an intense sincerity.

Elle was stunned, but absorbed the words intently. Never in their life had they thought of their coming out in that way. To Elle, their journey of discovery had felt like something other people had helped them make sense of. They had always been thankful to others, but not once had they ever thought to be thankful to themself. The idea of it rolled around in Elle's head. They felt comforted by the notion that being themself was a gift that Elle gave to themself each and every day.

"Thank you. Which I know you said not to do, but—I'll try," Elle said. As empowering as the thought was, though, Elle still had to ask the question that had been gnawing away at them. They bit their lip, closed their eyes, and let the words fly.

"And, umm . . . I know this is probably a lot to ask—but, well, you're still one of the *only* nonbinary people I've ever met. There's not really anyone else I can talk to about this stuff. So I wanted to ask, I've been having some trouble lately—with people at school and stuff. Some people, even when I tell them my name and pronouns, they just won't listen. They just *refuse* to see me as nonbinary. How do you deal with people like that? Is there something I could say to make them understand?" Elle tentatively asked, with desperate hope caught in their throat.

For the first time since Elle had started speaking to them, Nuri's dazzling smile slowly faded from their face. They ran their hand through their hair and let out a deep breath.

"Aww man, that's . . . that's quite the question you got there, Elle. Look, I wish there was an easy answer. I wish there was something you could say that would make all the bigots and jerks go away, but I don't think there is. You and me, we're smashing the binary, yeah?" Nuri said compassionately, though with the faintest twinge of sadness. Elle nodded, disappointed in what they were hearing but still hanging on Nuri's every word.

"And that makes us totally awesome wonder beings! But . . . some people don't like it when people are more than they understand.

And some people don't *want* to understand. But it's not your job to make them. Your job is just to keep being yourself, and not let them take away from the wonderful journey you're on," Nuri said as softly as a dawn's first ray of sunshine.

"I get it, but . . . so there's really no good way to stand up for yourself?" Elle asked. They knew their hero was offering wisdom and comfort, but it still felt bitter. Nuri cocked an eyebrow, an expressive gesture of playful curiosity that made them so magnetic on screen.

"Well, I didn't say that, now, did I? If you feel it's safe to do so, you should always feel free to stand up for yourself. And if some people *still* don't accept you? Then that's *their* loss. We're on a wide and wondrous spectrum that reaches out in every which way, Elle, and that's something worth celebrating with the world." Nuri's smile returned, and it was so infectious that Elle couldn't help but smile back.

"The way I look at it, who I am—it's not for anyone else, only myself. So whether it's how I present, how I choose what roles to audition for, or heck—even when I'm deciding on dinner, I try to follow my happiness. That's my *North Star* I can follow through the darkest of nights. When I have doubts about my identity, I just ask if being enby is what makes me feel the happiest. And if it is—which it always is—then what else really matters?" Nuri said.

Coming from them, it really did sound like a classic Phantom Thief inspiring heart-to-heart speech. Elle tried to commit every word to memory, like carvings in a stone. They wanted to be able to play the memory over and over in their mind. For once, it felt like Elle was really talking to someone who completely understood how they felt.

There was so much Elle wanted to discuss with Nuri, but they were keenly aware that they only had a few short, precious moments more. Already, a small line of people had formed, waiting for their chance to meet the star of the show. For this brief conversation, Elle didn't feel like they were going through their journey alone. Having to give up that connection so soon, it didn't feel fair.

"It's just . . . it's frustrating. You know? Feeling like I gotta figure this all out on my own," Elle whispered with a bitter edge.

"I know. Believe me, I know. I wish we had more guides, but I like to think that means we're free to define for ourselves who and how we want to be. You and me, we get to be *trailblazers* for everyone who comes after us. I dunno, kinda sounds like an adventure to me, don't you think?" Nuri warmly replied. Elle nodded in response, taking in Nuri's words of wisdom.

"Yeah . . . okay, yeah!" Elle said, excitement picking up in their voice. Nuri was right. This was an adventure, and Elle knew they had what it took to face it head-on. Nuri beamed with joy, and reached out their hand for the comic Elle was tightly clutching.

"So I think that if you just keep being your awesome self, everything's gonna be just fine. Deal?" Nuri said as they wrote in Elle's book with a gold-colored Sharpie pen.

"I will. I promise," Elle answered, taking back the signed comic book. Elle quickly flipped open the cover to see its new inscription. Inside the book now read:

Dear Elle,
Never forget how strong you are.
Keep following that North Star,
Nuri Grena

Elle felt like they read the note fifty times in a single second. Having this permanent memento of meeting their hero, their heart felt so full of glowing joy that they thought it might fly out of their body on magical wings made of sparkles. They almost began walking back toward Jerome when suddenly inspiration struck them. Elle turned back around to face Nuri.

"Sorry! One last thing. If it's okay, would you mind . . ." Elle leaned in closer to whisper their request to the *Phantom Thief* star. Nuri listened closely, and then nodded enthusiastically.

"Heck yeah I can do that! Let's do it. All right, got your phone ready to record me saying it?" they asked. Grena closed their eyes, took in a deep breath, and suddenly took on the cool, charismatic presence of their TV character. In a booming, dramatic voice they declared,

"Elle Campbell, I hereby induct you as a member of the Corporeal Crew. You are, from now until our paths double cross, an ally of the Phantom Thief!"

TWENTY

Stepping away from Nuri's table, Elle felt so light and free that it was like they were walking on clouds. They made their way back to Jerome, and lifted their signed comic to their face to try to hide the enormous smile that had overtaken them. Not that hiding their grin did any good; Elle's joy was visibly beaming off them.

"You get it signed?" Jerome asked them with anticipation. Elle wasn't sure they could articulate words more advanced than an overexcited scream, so they vigorously nodded their head up and down.

"That's what I'm talking about!" Jerome pumped his fist and held up his palm for a high five. In the past, Elle would have ignored Jerome's friendliness, or responded with a sullen eye roll. But Jerome had been there for them today. He could have easily gotten Elle in trouble, or let them freeze up in front of Nuri, but he hadn't. When Elle had needed support, he had been there to give it, no questions asked. Elle decided then and there that it was time they started returning the kindness that they had been given. They jumped up and smacked Jerome's outstretched hand with as much force and energy as they could muster.

"So, you get what you were hoping for out of this? You talked to them about what you needed to talk about?" he asked Elle.

"Yeah. I think I did. There's a lot more to figure out, I think. But that's okay too," Elle replied softly. Jerome knelt down so he could look Elle in the eye, and put a hand on their shoulder.

"Hey, I want you to know—I can't fully understand what it is you're going through, but for what it's worth, I'm really dang proud of you. At your age, it's not easy being yourself. But you're *fighting* for it, and it's amazing. Long as you're fighting in that ring, I want to be in your corner. Ya get me?" he said in a tone as warm as a big cotton blanket.

"I mean, I don't fully understand the parts that I think were boxing lingo? But I get what you mean. Thank you," Elle said.

"How 'bout I take the comic, though," Jerome said, reaching to take what was now Elle's most valuable possession in the world.

"Gonna be hard explaining to your mom how you got your hands on a brand-new comic while stuck in a detention room," he said. As reluctant as Elle was to part with the book, they knew Jerome's logic was sound.

"Hey, how come you're helping cover for me? Why didn't you tell Mom when you saw me in line?" Elle asked.

For once, it was Jerome's turn to roll his eyes at Elle. "Pfft! You kidding me? 'In line.' Child, I saw you all the way back at the café hiding behind the chair!" he told Elle in a matter-of-fact way. Elle's jaw fell with utter shock. After all they had done to stay hidden, they couldn't believe what they were hearing.

"Huh?! You knew I was there? But—but why didn't you say any-thing? You knew, but how come—" Elle nervously stammered before Jerome cut them off.

"What kind of narc do you think I am? You really think I'd go tattling on you for *this*? I think it's awesome you got outta detention!"

"You do?" Elle asked with surprise.

"Absolutely! A day stuck spent locked in a room does nobody no good. Day like today, breaking the rules, meeting your hero, having fun with your friends—smart move having them distract your mom, by the way. Love to see that teamwork—you're gonna remember today for the rest of your life." Elle was moved by Jerome's kindness. Suddenly, they were regretting all the times they had been so standoffish to him.

"Jerome, I'm . . . I'm sorry. You've always been really nice to me, and I guess I kinda . . . haven't," said an embarrassed Elle.

Jerome waved away Elle's apology. "Aww, don't worry. I get it. My parents split up when I was around your age, and I was a downright *terror* to anyone my mom tried to date. I'd tell you stories, but I don't wanna give you any ideas."

Elle felt unable to meet Jerome's gaze, and their eyes darted around the room as they tried to think of a way to return his kindness. "Hey—umm, Jerome. Maybe tonight, would you . . . would you wanna watch a movie with me after dinner?" they said slowly. Going out of their way to interact with their mother's boyfriend wasn't within Elle's comfort zone, but they wanted to try. "Cheery" was how Elle would describe Jerome's default state, but now they were positively overjoyed. He looked thrilled that Elle wanted to connect with him, and Elle felt a bitter pang of regret that they had kept Jerome at arm's length for so long.

"Absolutely! I got just the movie for you. The guy has a chain saw for a hand and he's fighting demons during knights and castles times, you're gonna love it," Jerome replied, making no attempt to hide his celebratory excitement. "I'll have the popcorn ready at eight p.m. sharp!" Jerome was all smiles as he held up his watch to Elle.

Elle hadn't been paying attention to the time, and the sight of Jerome's watch sent a frigid wave of terror down their back. They grabbed Jerome's wrist and pulled it closer to them. To Elle's stunned horror, the ticking hands of the clock revealed that a mere twenty minutes was all that stood between them and the end of detention. Elle's heart was beating at a mile a minute, and they would need to move just as fast if they had any hope of making it back to school without getting caught.

"Oh no! Detention is almost over. I have to get outta here!" Elle said in a hurried panic.

"I'll keep your mom here, try to buy you a few extra minutes. Now get going!" Jerome ordered. His expression had turned deathly serious. The two traded knowing nods, and Elle bolted down the shelves of books, racing toward the exit.

✿ ✿ ✿

When Elle burst through the doors of the Purple Prose bookshop, Taylor and Agatha were already waiting for them outside. They'd barely made it two steps before their friends began their supportive yet overwhelming barrage of questions.

"How'd it go?"

"Did you meet them?"

"What'd you talk about?"

"Did you get something signed?"

"What'd they smell like?"

Elle didn't have time to stop moving and talk with Taylor and Agatha, so they tried their best to gather their thoughts and respond on the go.

"Great, yes, mostly gender stuff, yes, and I dunno . . . vanilla?" Elle answered between moderately out-of-breath pants. If they were already this winded from sprinting across the bookstore, how in the heck were they supposed to get back to school in time?

"Yes! I *knew* it would be vanilla. Told you, Ags. Get out of here with your honey lilac *nonsense*," Taylor triumphantly celebrated. Agatha gave him a playful jab on the shoulder, and picked up her pace to catch up with Elle.

"Let the record show that me and Taylor absolutely *crushed* Operation Distract Mama C," Agatha bragged, more than a little proud of herself.

"Please never refer to my mom as 'Mama C' again," Elle responded bluntly. Elle speed walked across the parking lot toward where the trio had left their scooters. Elle had no idea how they were going to make it across town in time, but they had to try.

"Okay, if she's not there already, Ms. Fambro will be coming back to detention really soon. I love y'all, but I gotta go *now*," Elle explained to their friends. They looked around the downtown area, trying to mentally map out the fastest route for them to take. While Elle was lost in a nervous panic, Taylor gripped the handle of their scooter.

"I mean, if you need to go *fast*, I got an idea . . ." Taylor said with the kind of mischievous, sharklike grin that was normally Agatha's specialty. Elle swallowed a gulp; they knew exactly what Taylor was suggesting, and they knew they didn't have any better options.

"You don't mean . . ." Elle asked, already knowing the answer. Taylor nodded with excited glee.

"You gotta go down Hank's Hill!"

❁ ❁ ❁

It took only a moment to get from the Purple Prose to the steep, imposing incline that was Hank's Hill. From the top, Elle peered over the edge. The curving cement path had claimed many an over-confident skateboarder and bicyclist. Running over a pebble or hitting a pothole was all it would take to send Elle hurtling off their scooter.

"There's got to be another way," they said, looking down and gripping their handlebars tightly in fear.

"It *is* the most direct route back to school," Agatha offered, though the pained look on her face as she gazed down the hill was more revealing of her true feelings.

"And you go down and it'll turn you into *superspeed* and you can *fwoosh* back in no time," added a hyperactive Taylor.

"Or if you botch it and eat concrete, all your broken bones will make detention seem like no big deal," Agatha said, offering what Elle supposed would pass as support. Elle took in a deep breath: It was now or never. They weren't sure they could do this, but they reminded themself of their talk with Nuri. If Nuri believed that Elle really was courageous enough to take on anything, then they could believe it too. Before they could take off, though, they still had one important thing left to do. Without warning, Elle turned toward their friends, and wrapped each of them in a hug.

"You guys, thank you. For everything. For busting me out of detention and spending today with me and coming to the signing. You both made today *really special*. This was the *best* Saturday. I'm lucky to have you as friends," they said to Taylor and Agatha with heartfelt warmness.

"You really are. Just remember, little flower, you owe me next time I need help with something witchy and-slash-or potentially a crime," Agatha called out.

"Aww, it was fun! I'll break out of teacher jail with you any day, Elle-dorado!" Taylor cheerfully responded.

"I'll text ya when I get home!" Elle promised as they kicked off the pavement and started their descent down the dreaded Hank's Hill. Within seconds, their scooter had accelerated to blistering speeds. The turn for the arcade zoomed by in the blink of an eye, and telephone poles, street signs, and barren trees whizzed past them in a dizzying blur. Elle was suddenly aware that they weren't wearing any helmet or pads. One wrong move, one fall—and they could end up breaking as easily as the gnarled branches of the trees they were racing past. But there was no turning back now. They had committed to it. Either they were going to make it back on time, or they were going to give it their absolute all trying.

As Elle rounded a bend in the road, it took all their effort to steer the scooter and keep it steady. Their ears were full with the roaring screeches of wheel against road. Elle had never gone this fast before. As terrifying as it was, they were indeed crossing the town more quickly than they had even hoped for. Already, Elle could see the redbrick exterior of the M. Sara Museum of Art rapidly getting closer. Elle smirked thinking about their recent ban from the museum. According to the worker who may or may not be an owl spirit, whizzing past the outside was the closest they could get to it now. Well, at least until mid-January.

Elle needed to keep their focus on the sidewalk ahead of them if they didn't want to take a tumble, but something they saw out of the corner of their eye demanded their attention. Sitting on the hood of a car parked on the street outside the redbrick building was the museum guide herself, happily helping herself to the container of ice cream that Elle and their friends had stolen earlier that day. After all her protests about not daring to eat the ice cream lest it besmirch the sanctity of art, Elle quite enjoyed the sight of catching her red-handed. Or, to be more accurate given the mint chocolate chip, green-spooned.

"I knew it!" they called out with smug satisfaction as they raced by in a blur. Elle had no time to look back and see the museum guide's reaction; they had to keep moving. They took in a deep breath, and kicked off the pavement as hard as they could. Elle needed to try to regain some of the speed they'd lost since the road had flattened out.

However, the farther Elle traveled, the more tired they were becoming. Their leg felt like it was on fire, and every kick off the ground to build speed was like firecrackers were going off inside them. Elle was too tired to have any thoughts other than the drive to keep moving.

They had only ten minutes left before detention was over, but if they dug deep and gritted through it, they still had a chance to make it back in time. As they kept going down the sidewalk, a gigantic statue of a baseball became visible over the trees. Seeing the familiar sight of Johnny Baseball's Hot Dogs & Home Runs gave Elle a sorely needed boost of encouragement. They really were getting closer!

Feeling newfound energy, Elle picked up speed as they approached the hot dog restaurant. Right before they could pass by, though, the doors opened, and out walked Johnny Baseball himself. The giant baseball-headed mascot was bringing out a tray full of chili dogs and lemonade. He was right in Elle's path, and they were too close and going too fast to stop or steer away.

"Look out!" Elle yelled in warning. Johnny Baseball looked up to see Elle barreling toward him on their scooter. He tried to dart out of the way, but was hampered by the tray of food and his own gigantic foam head. The mascot tripped over his own feet, and fumbled the tray. Hot dogs flopped in the air and chili splashed across his baseball face.

"Sorry!" Elle called out apologetically to the fallen mascot as they scootered away. Elle only briefly took their eye off the road ahead in order to look down and make sure no chili had landed on their dress. After all the day's adventures, though, the green gown was miraculously still clean.

Soon, Elle was turning into the cul-de-sac from which they had first gotten their scooter, in the faraway times of earlier in the morning. Elle zipped through the tranquil neighborhood, past manicured lawns and idyllic homes. Ahead of them lay the thin strip of woods that separated the neighborhood from the school. Elle looked around, and spotted the pair of off-putting children they had traded with playing at the end of the block. Elle wasn't sure why their faces were painted like tigers, or why they were fighting with lit sparklers taped to foam swords, but the weird games of elementary schoolers would just have to be a mystery.

As Elle approached the end of the road, they only barely slowed down the tiniest bit. Instead of stopping, they leapt off the scooter. Elle landed on both feet in the grass, and used the momentum of the scooter to instantly start running at top speed.

"Hi, creepy kids! Bye, creepy kids!" Elle said to the two children, who looked at the scooter Elle had dropped in front of them with unnervingly blank expressions. Seconds later, Elle passed through the line of trees that would lead them back to school. They bobbed and weaved around roots and rocks and branches. Forget baseball or capoeira, getting back to school was proving to be by far the most intense exercise of Elle's life. Their legs were aching, and there was a cramp in their side that felt like lobsters were pinching their stomach. But the school was within sight now; they just had to hang on a little longer. To get the one last boost they needed, Elle hummed the theme song to *Phantom Thief* to spur themself on. Just when they thought they couldn't go any farther, Elle finally reached the edge and the woods. Every muscle in their body ached, but they had never been so deeply relieved to be back at Broderick Middle School.

Elle quickly checked the time on their phone: They only had three minutes left! They crouched down, and started sneaking their way across the school's parking lot. They remembered where Fambro had been sleeping in her car, and hid behind a nearby minivan to see if she was still there. If Taylor had been wrong, if Fambro had gone back to the room before detention was over, there was nothing Elle would be able to do to avoid detention for a month. Fortunately, Elle had arrived just in time. The less-than-perfectly-responsible teacher had just gotten out of her car, and was twisting her arms to the sky to stretch away the stiffness from her nap. After finishing, Fambro pulled out her cell phone and started walking back to the school. Elle had to navigate around the minivan to make sure they were staying out of the teacher's view.

"Hi, babe. Yeah, I'm headed back in now," Elle overheard Ms. Fambro say into her phone.

"No, it's not ridiculous. What's ridiculous is making me come in on Saturdays. It's as much a punishment for me as it is for the kids. They probably spent the whole time playing games or watching movies on their phone. I bet you I did them a favor by taking a nap. Yeah, I'll make reservations for dinner tonight. Yes, I promise it'll be fancier this time than the pizza place with the arcade," said Ms. Fambro, continuing her phone call as she headed to the school's entrance. As soon as the teacher walked through the doors, Elle broke out in a sprint around the school building.

With Fambro in the school, there was only one way that Elle was going to make it back to the classroom first. They would need to climb through the window. The marching band had long since finished their practice, so Elle could now sneak back in through the classroom window without being seen. Elle's face lit up with joy when they saw the large, box-shaped air-conditioning unit that would be their stepping stool to getting inside. Summoning the last ounces of strength that they didn't even know they had, Elle hoisted themself atop the metallic box. They squeezed through the narrow window, and landed with a tumble back in the empty detention room.

Finally able to stop and catch their breath, the relief Elle felt was nothing short of monumental. They had done it. Elle had broken out, met their hero, and gotten back without anyone knowing. Well, without anyone but Jerome and Casey knowing, but that was okay. Letting out a relaxed chuckle of contentment, Elle could have spent the rest of the day lying on that classroom floor, savoring their accomplishment. But celebrations would have to wait. They could already hear the *clickety-tap* sounds of Ms. Fambro's high heels echoing from the hallway. Elle quickly picked themself up off the floor and rushed to their desk. They breathed out a sigh of relief when they sat down. But that relief only lasted for a brief second, until Elle noticed that the flamboyantly dressed mannequin decoy was still sitting in the desk next to them. Elle's felt like they were on a roller coaster of emotions, and joy had just done a loop-the-loop into utter panic.

Elle grabbed the mannequin and rushed back to the window. Shoving a theater prop out a second-story window wasn't the *best* plan, but they didn't have time for anything else. They pushed and pushed, and finally managed to get the vaguely Elle-shaped chunk of plastic out the window. Elle heard it land on the air conditioner with a satisfying *CHUNK* sound. Or at least, they had heard *most* of the mannequin fall out the window. Elle looked down at the ground to find that a plastic arm had popped off the doll while Elle had been struggling with it. They reached down for it, but just then, the classroom doorknob began to turn. In less than a second, Elle would be face-to-face with Ms. Fambro. Elle quickly snatched the arm off the ground and hid it behind their back at the exact moment Fambro entered the room.

"Ms. Fambro! You're back! Is detention over already?" Elle asked the teacher, fake innocence dripping from their voice. For a moment, Fambro didn't say a word; she simply looked at Elle with an untrusting eye.

"Hey there, Campbell. Yup, detention's over. What's that you're up to? I left you here on your own, but you know you should stay in your seat," she said disapprovingly. Elle simply smiled in face of Fambro's suspicions. They'd come too far to get caught because of a lousy poker face.

"Oh, I'm sorry. It's just—does the air in here feel *stuffy* to you? Ugh, so dry," Elle said sweetly while inching backward toward the open window.

"It was making me cough, so I thought I'd get some fresh air in and try to . . ." they continued. While still facing Ms. Fambro, Elle dropped the plastic arm out the window behind them.

"COUGH COUGH," Elle faked as loud as they could to cover the clang of the mannequin arm hitting the AC unit. It seemed to have done the trick, as Fambro threw up her hands and turned toward the door.

"Well, you have officially served your time. Get on outta this stuffy room and drink some water. You're free!" Fambro announced. Hearing those words, it took all of Elle's willpower not to explode with celebration right then and there. They'd started gathering their things when the teacher called out to them one more time.

"Hey, I know this wasn't fun being there. For what it's worth, I'm sorry you lost your Saturday."

"Don't worry about it," Elle said with a smile.

"I made the most of it."

ACKNOWLEDGMENTS

TK

ABOUT THE AUTHOR

After a number of years working in game design, Ben Kahn began their journey as a published author in 2015. Initially focused on writing comic books, Kahn's work received critical praise, including nominations for the Ignatz Award for Outstanding Series and the GLAAD Media Award for Original Graphic Novel. With *Elle Campbell Wins Their Weekend*, Kahn makes their debut in the exciting world of prose. When not writing, Ben continues their never-ending quest of self-discovery alongside their partner and the cuddliest kitty around.